Books by Thomas Locke

The Spectrum Chronicles

3

Path Finder

Thomas Locke

BETHANY HOUSE PUBLISHERS
MINNEAPOLIS, MINNESOTA 55438

Cover illustration by Joe Nordstrom

Published by Bethany House Publishers
A Ministry of Bethany Fellowship, Inc.
11300 Hampshire Avenue South
Minneapolis, Minnesota 55438

Printed in the United States of America.

Library of Congress Cataloging-in-Publication Data

Locke, Thomas.
    Path finder / Thomas Locke.
      p.   cm. — (The spectrum chronicles ; bk. 3)
    Summary: Consuela's attempt to rescue her friend Wander, who is being held hostage, takes her on a secret mission on a renegade spaceship.

    [1. Science fiction.] I. Title. II. Series: Locke, Thomas. Spectrum chronicles ; 3.
PZ7.L7945Pat   1995
[Fic]—dc20   95–473
ISBN 1–55661–434–9   CIP
                                       AC

FOR PETE AND ANNE PIERCE

*May your life together be enriched with joy
and blessed with the adventure of love.*

THOMAS LOCKE is a delightful addition to Bethany's team of writers. His exceptional creativity has taken flight in this latest book for teens, the third in THE SPECTRUM CHRONICLES. An avid fantasy and science-fiction reader himself, Thomas Locke offers the young adult audience a thrill-packed tale with a spiritual message that spans both worlds.

– ONE –

Consuela did not have much time.

The realization struck her as soon as she stepped into her living room. She could not say how she knew, but the certainty was there, and it sped her actions. Not to mention attaching wings to her heart.

The entire time she tried to talk through her mother's alcoholic fog, part of her mind remained fastened upon the thought that she would soon be back with Wander. The surging thrill lifted her beyond her mother's muddled bewilderment, beyond her own pain of loss and departure. For this time there was a sense of belonging elsewhere, tied to this new mysterious place by her love for a man. A sensitive, openhearted, talented young man. One who truly cared for her.

The last thing she remembered, she and Wander had been counting down their ship's approach along the lightwave. A pirate ship had been hovering just down the shadowlane, powered up and ready to pounce. Then the first ball of deadly blue energy had been flung across the space dividing them, and her world had exploded into a billion painfully shimmering bits.

Then she had woken up in her own bed, at home in Baltimore.

"Mama, are you listening to me?"

"Of course I am. Don't ask silly questions." Her mother's words were slurred, and her eyes remained glued to the television.

The bland voices of soap-opera stars mouthed lines that made no sense whatsoever to Consuela. She resisted the urge to walk over and turn off the set, knowing from experience that it would only start an argument. "I'm going away for a while. I have to. There's something important I need to do."

"She goes off and leaves me, doesn't say a word," her mother mumbled, drink and self-pity oiling her voice.

"That's why I came back, Mama, to tell you." Speaking to her mother as to a little child. Knowing this was required. Part of her mind felt the unexplained pressing need to hurry, to finish here and move on, to get the message through her mother's self-imposed fog. Another part registered the fact that it was earlier in the day than usual for Consuela's mother to be this far along, and that her complexion was pastier than normal. Consuela felt a stab of guilt. Maybe this was her mother's way of dealing with Consuela's absence, by drinking even more than usual.

She grasped hold of her mother's arm, said softly, "I had to come back, Mama. I had to tell you how much I love you."

A bleary gaze turned her way. The glass was shifted to her lap, and a hand patted her own. "You always were my good little girl."

"I've tried hard to do right, Mama," Consuela said. "That's why I need to be going."

"Go and leave me all alone." Her mother's self-pitying tone returned as she fumbled for her glass. "Doesn't matter what happens to her own mother."

"It does so matter, Mama. It matters a lot." But Consuela was forced to watch as her mother subsided into disjointed mutterings, her rheumy eyes glued to the television screen. Consuela remained kneeling beside her mother's chair until her legs ached, talking softly from time to time. But her mother did not respond.

Finally Consuela rose to her feet and walked into the kitchen. The number was still there, scrawled in a child's hand on the wall beside the phone. Daniel answered before the first ring was finished.

"Just like always," Consuela said, a sudden rush of relief tightening her throat. "There and waiting whenever I need you."

"Consuela!" The joy shouted across the distance. "Bliss, it's Consuela! Wait, wait, don't say anything, she's running to pick up the extension."

The phone clicked a second time, then a faintly accented voice like chiming bells asked, "Where are you?"

"Back home," Consuela said, finding enormous comfort in not being alone. "I just came back."

"This is great," Daniel gushed. "My company is opening a branch in Baltimore, and they're assigning me to run it."

"It's a big promotion," Bliss added.

"We're waiting for the movers to arrive," Daniel went on. "I thought that was who was calling."

"Did it go well, my dear?" Bliss asked.

"Yes. Very." Consuela took a breath. "But it's not over. I have to go back."

There was a long pause on the other end, then Daniel spoke, more subdued now. "Is it bad?"

"I'm not sure. Not for me, anyway. Not now. Well, our ship got hit by pirates, and that was awful. It felt as if my mind were going to explode. And I need to go back and make sure Wander is okay."

Bliss asked, "Who?"

"Maybe it would be better," Daniel said, "if you took it from the top."

So she did, hastily explaining how she had woken up in a snow-covered field to find herself facing the spaceport launching pad, hearing voices in her head, accompanied by a young apprentice scout named Wander.

Bliss interrupted, "Did you say spaceport, dear?"

Dan asked, "Apprentice what?"

"Scout. And his name is Wander." Feeling a little catch in her breath at the sound of his name. Rushing on, still caught by the invisible pressure to complete her tasks and return. Hoping it was going to be possible, despite the worry she felt for her mother, knowing that she *needed* to return.

When she was finished, there was another long silence before Dan finally said, "If I didn't know you, I'd say you needed to go wake up again."

"It's no stranger than the story you told me after we met," Bliss reminded him.

"No, I suppose not." He mused a moment longer, then said, "So you think you should go back?"

"I *have* to."

"What do you want us to do?"

The simple question flooded her with relief. Here were people she could trust. People who believed in her to the point where the impossible was accepted as fact, and who would help her face whatever came. Here were friends. "I'm worried about Mom," Consuela said, and hastily described her mother's state. "Could you stop by and check on her?"

"Consider it done," Daniel replied.

"Thanks. Thanks a lot." Thunder rumbled through the kitchen window. For some reason Consuela felt the tingling pressure to move. "I've got to go."

"What's the rush?"

"I'm not sure, but I feel as though I've got to *hurry*."

"Then you probably do," Daniel said. "Think you can spare a moment for prayer?"

Consuela bowed her head, listened to Daniel intone the words, and felt an answering call within her heart. One that echoed the same sense of awe and silent longing she had experienced during transition. A silent voice spoke to her heart with something far beyond mere words. An invitation so gentle she could have ignored it if she wished, and yet granted with such power that her entire being resonated.

When Daniel stopped speaking, Consuela remained silent and still, feeling the comforting need without understanding what it was. Then the thunder rumbled once more, and the tingling sense of pressure brought her back.

"I have to go," she said quietly.

"We will be praying for you," Bliss said solemnly. "Each and every day."

———

She had never been in a house that big before.

Under other circumstances, she would have loved to walk around and gawk. But there was no time for sightseeing, and the treatment she was receiving was bringing her to a slow boil.

To begin with, the maid had left her standing alone in the front hall until Rick's mother had appeared and looked her up and down and asked her how she happened to know Rick. The news that Rick had been dating her the night of his disappearance was greeted with a disdainful sniff.

"I know all of my son's little friends," Rick's mother replied. "I am positive I have never heard him mention you before."

Consuela tried to hold her rising temper. "I assure you, Mrs. Reynolds, I had a date with Rick."

"Be that as it may," the woman replied, "Rick did not disappear over the weekend as you say. It was on a week-night, a Monday to be precise."

"Of course," Consuela said. "He told me he went back to the carnival with Daniel after I didn't show up at school."

The woman's glacial gaze sharpened. "How did you know about the carnival? Have you spoken to the police?"

"I told you, I was there."

The woman gave her another up-and-down inspection, then spun on her heel and started up the curving stairway. "Wait there."

Consuela stood and listened to the woman go from room to room, calling for someone named Henry. She stared up at the glistening chandelier, then inspected the life-size family portrait with its oh-so-proper dress and smiles and postures, and decided maybe Rick didn't have it all so perfect after all.

When the woman returned, she was accompanied by a tall, heavyset replica of Rick. Consuela watched them descend the double-bannistered stairway as though on parade. "This is the young woman I was telling you about."

The man's tone was rich and resonant and very condescending. "What's this about you and Rick and that carnival?"

The thunder boomed again, echoing through the vast hall with its lofty ceilings and marble flooring and sterile unloving atmosphere. Consuela felt as though the approaching storm was calling to her, urging her to finish her work and leave. "I just came by to tell you that I've seen Rick and he's fine."

"Now look here." The man stepped forward close enough to tower over her and bear down. "If you know anything about my son's whereabouts, I want you to tell me, and tell me *now*."

"Perhaps we should call the police," the woman suggested.

"Plenty of time for that." Her husband was growing increasingly red in the face. "First I intend to get to the bottom of this myself."

Consuela stood her ground. "I can't tell you where he is because I don't know. Not exactly. But I can tell you he's doing fine."

"Then why doesn't he come home?" the woman demanded. "Has he been kidnapped?"

Consuela inspected Rick's mother. There was far more irritation than concern in her features. "Rick is fine. He is just caught up in an adventure. He'll be home as soon as it's over."

"Nonsense," the man snapped. "He has made an absolute shambles of his responsibilities right here. How could our son embarrass us this way? How could he let down the family name? Doesn't he have a shred of decency?"

Thunder boomed outside, and the sense of urgency grew so strong Consuela felt as though she no longer had any choice.

"Rick is fine," she said, turning and making for the door. "That's all I can tell you. He doesn't want you to worry. He'll be home as soon as he can."

Consuela fled out the great entrance, their cries of protest flung skyward with the growing wind. She raced across the road and through a broad park. Overhead the trees waved their branches, urging her to ever greater speed.

At the park's other side was a wide intersection, and beside it a bus stop and telephone booth. Consuela bounded inside, closed the door against the dust and wind and rumbling thunderclaps. Lightning sparked across the cloudswept horizon as she looked up the school's number, deposited the coins, and dialed with fingers made clumsy with haste.

When the school secretary answered, Consuela deepened her voice and pretended to be her mother, as she had been forced to do on many other occasions. She assured the school secretary that everything was all right, that her daughter was fine now; yes, she had indeed been ill, but she was doing much better, and they had decided that she should take a trip up into the mountains to stay with friends for a while to recover fully. How long? Consuela hedged and promised that as soon as the girl was back to full health she would be returning to school. Yes, of course, she understood that a letter and doctor's report should have been sent, but she had been so very busy with work and tending to her sick daughter that the letter had slipped her mind. Yes, of course, she would give her daughter everyone's best wishes for her speedy recovery.

Consuela set down the phone just as lightning blasted down so close that the light and the sound struck her almost at the same moment. Urged on by pressures she neither understood nor questioned, Consuela flung open the door and raced back into the park. Another bolt of lightning struck close behind her, urging her on.

At the park's center clearing, a blast of wind struck her with such force that she had no choice but to stop. She squinted through the swirling cloud of dust and leaves and saw that the clouds seemed to be encircling her, looming bigger and closer and darker, their gray-black surface illuminated by great internal sparks. Thunderbolts roared on all sides, splitting the air with such force that little answering flickers of static electricity began glimmering from her arms and legs and dress. The lightning seemed to stalk her, moving ever closer, and yet the closer it came, the dimmer the sound became, as though the light and the concentrated force were pushing her away, farther and farther away until even as the lightning bolt crashed down right where she thought she had been standing, she was no longer there.

–Two–

Consuela awoke with a gasp. Her first thread of awareness grew into a shocking world of white and stringent
smells. She shut her eyes, took a shaky breath, felt the alien
odors biting at her nostrils. Opening her eyes once more,
she forced the room into focus and saw herself surrounded
by instruments and dials and softly beeping noises.

A hospital. Although nothing she saw looked familiar,
still there was no mistaking the overly clean environment,
the soft erasing of all outside noise, the absence of any per-
sonal touches to the room. Consuela struggled up on one
elbow, looked about the windowless chamber, felt panic
rising with her wakefulness.

She was back, and she was alone.

"Wander?"

The room swept up her voice along with all other
sounds, replying only with a soft sibilant sigh. Consuela
struggled upright. She ignored the faint pinging from a ma-
chine on her headboard when she stripped off the band of
wires attached to her wrist. She swung her feet to the floor,
found a pair of disposable slippers there waiting for her.

"Wander?" Slowly she rose to her feet, grasping the

bed's side rail with both hands. Her legs seemed barely able to support her weight. "Can anybody hear me?"

She felt a faint draft, reached behind herself with one hand, and groaned with frustration. There she was on the back of beyond, and they still had not come up with anything better than a hospital shift that left her backside exposed. Consuela forced her faltering legs to carry her over to the narrow closet, where to her vast relief she found a terry cloth robe.

She had barely slipped it around her when the door slid back to admit a bright-eyed young woman who could not have been much older than Consuela. "It is not permitted for the young lady to arise," she said, her voice carrying a lilting accent.

"Where is Wander?" Consuela demanded, her strength too meager to permit small talk. "For that matter, where am I?"

"You are on Avanti," the white-clad nurse replied. "Welcome to my home. As for this Wander, I am sure if you kindly wait in bed for the doctor, he—"

"Was there a young man brought in with me?"

"There were several brought off the ship." Her eyes glimmered with admiration. "All Avanti knows of your battle with the pirates. You are heroes."

Consuela started for the door, but her legs chose that moment to falter. She would have collapsed if the nurse had not been there to catch her. "Please, you must return to bed," the nurse urged her. "You must show a kindness to your body. You have been unconscious for six days."

So long? Consuela allowed her fears to surface. "A man my age, a scout. Slender—"

"Tall and fair with most handsome features," the nurse gaily agreed, gently guiding her back toward the bed. "Of course I know this Wander. He and you are the only two who have not fully recovered."

Consuela used the last remaining fragments of her strength to halt her progress toward the bed, grip the nurse's arm, and plead, "Take me to him."

The nurse inspected her with excited eyes. "He is your special man?"

"Very special," Consuela agreed.

Clearly the idea of furthering a hospital romance met with the nurse's approval. "You will please sit. I will find a coaster and return."

Confused by the unfamiliar words, but relieved by her evident agreement, Consuela permitted the nurse to guide her down. She watched the nurse then turn and leave, too tired to even protest at being left alone.

Soon enough the nurse returned, pushing in front of her what appeared to be a wheelchair without wheels. "Here, you are to please sit," she said, drawing the floating apparatus up alongside the bed. With an expert efficiency of motion, she eased Consuela off the bed and onto the chair.

"Oooh, wonderful," Consuela sighed. Not only did the chair take her weight, but it actually took weight from her. She felt light as a feather, barely heavy enough to remain in the chair and not float away.

"Yes, is very nice. Sometimes when I am tired I use the coaster for little restings," the nurse agreed. She spun the chair about and pushed her through the doorway.

Outside, the hallway was fairly crowded, and everywhere faces greeted Consuela with smiles. The attention left her feeling very uncomfortable. When they passed through an empty space, she said, "Does everybody around here know who I am?"

"All Avanti knows," the nurse cheerfully agreed. "Every day is report on newscast of how you progress. I come off duty and meet hundreds of reporters. All want to hear how

beautiful scout lady and handsome scout man are pro-
gressing." She gave an excited little sigh. "And now we are
finding that he is your special man. Whole world will want
to hear how you sleep for six days, then cannot even wait
for doctor before seeking the handsome scout."

Consuela felt her cheeks growing red. "Is he all right?"

"Oh yes, monitors show all normal signs. But still he
sleeps." The nurse's bright face leaned into view. "Perhaps
he wakes for you, no? Oh, is all so romantic!"

The nurse stopped before a door marked with a yellow
warning shield and pressed in a code on the numerical
lock. When the door had sighed open, she pushed Consuela
inside.

Consuela could not help herself. When Wander came
into view, she gave a little gasp, partly of relief over seeing
him again, and partly over how pale and still he looked.
With his closed eyes and color only barely deeper than the
starched sheet, Wander looked like a little boy, helpless and
frail and utterly in need.

The nurse pushed Consuela over. She leaned forward
and grasped his hand. "His skin is so cold."

"Six days he sleeps," the nurse agreed. "The pirate attack, it was terrible, no? And you, a *sensitive* attached to
the ship's amplifiers, it was a wonder you survived."

Consuela turned to her in confusion. "You know all
about that?"

"All Avanti knows," the nurse repeated. "My world, we
suffer for years from pirate attacks on the shipping lanes.
Some years, only two or three ships come through. Slowly,
slowly we are strangled. We plead to the Hegemony for
help, and they do nothing." Her dark eyes scattered thrilling sparks about the room. "And suddenly in our skies appears a ship, and with it comes news that they bring with
them a captured pirate ship! And the captain tells how they

carry sensitives who find the shadowlanes, and tell of ship waiting to attack. So all Avanti waits to hear of scouts' recovery."

Consuela turned her attention back to Wander's sleeping form. She leaned forward, traced a finger down the side of his cheek. She was embarrassed by the nurse's closeness and her melodramatic interest. Still, she kissed his cheek and whispered, "Wander, it's Consuela. Can you hear me?"

The slumbering young man emitted a soft groan.

All concern for the nurse's unbridled interest vanished. Consuela raised herself up, although it was hard, for moving from the chair meant taking on her full weight. She leaned forward and kissed his forehead, his cheek, his lips. "Wake up, Wander. Please, for me. Open your eyes."

And he did.

Wander blinked and focused, seeing her and sighing with the pleasure that flooded his face. He whispered, "I dreamed you had left me. Gone back."

"I did," she said, matching his gentle tone. Raising his hand to cradle it against her chest, her other hand resting featherlight against his cheek. "But I came back."

Wander licked dry lips, managed, "For me?"

The wings of her heart fluttered against her ribs as she nodded and softly replied, "For you."

"Ooooh." The sound of the little nurse clapping hands together under her chin turned them both about. "Is just toooo wonderful. All Avanti will sing of this love. Wait, wait, I must go and find doctor." With that, the nurse spun around and was gone.

Wander returned his gaze to her and asked, "What was that all about?"

"Later," she said. She brushed the hair from his forehead, etching the memory of each feature on the surface of her heart. "Can I get you something?"

"Water."

She helped him drink, then drank herself. Consuela felt energy course through her with the liquid. She drained the cup, set it down, asked, "How do you—"

The door sighed open, and a familiar voice said, "Here they are. Just as I suspected. Planning more mischief, no doubt."

Consuela spun about. "Captain Arnol!"

The nurse squeezed past the captain and attempted to bar the doorway with her small frame. "No, no, is forbidden!"

"Silence," the captain snapped, and brusquely pushed the squawking nurse to one side. He stepped in, then turned and motioned for a stern black-robed figure to enter. "If you please, Diplomat."

"This room is off limits," the nurse squawked, her arms making frantic motions, trying to shoo the pair back out and away. "Only with doctor's orders can you enter here."

"Oh, do be quiet, that's a good little girl." The silver-maned diplomat swept into the room with the air of one long used to regal command.

"I am going for doctor," the nurse announced hotly, and fled.

"An excellent notion," the diplomat drawled. He bent over the bed and examined Wander with the coldest eyes Consuela had ever seen. "So this is the renegade scout."

"I assure you, Diplomat," Captain Arnol began from his post by the door. "I had no idea whatsoever—"

"Quite, quite." His eyes lifted to fasten Consuela with a gaze that held no pity, no compassion, no life. "And whom do we have here?"

"Oh, the girl." Arnol shrugged his unconcern. "Grimson sent her along as a trainee. Goodness only knows why. Her ability is scarcely measurable."

"Not another Talent then," the diplomat said, showing a trace of regret.

"Her?" Captain Arnol clearly found that humorous. "Whatever gave you that idea?"

"Yes, of course. Two Talents found together would be impossible, even for Senior Pilot Grimson." The glacial eyes swung back to the silent figure on the bed, and the tone sharpened. "What is your name, renegade?"

"My name is Wander," he replied, as hotly as his weakened state would allow. "But I am not a renegade, and I resent you calling me one."

"Resent, do you?" The diplomat sniffed his amusement. "Have you any idea with whom you speak?"

"I do not, nor do I care."

"You will show proper respect when addressing the diplomat, Scout Wander," Arnol barked.

"Peace." The diplomat raised one languid hand in dismissal. "The gallant scout will have ample time to learn respect and a myriad of other things once we have him properly settled."

Consuela shifted so that she came between the diplomat's gaze and Wander. "Where are you taking him?"

Eyes the color of a frozen sky rose to meet her own. Consuela struggled not to show the fear she felt. Something must have been revealed, however, for the diplomat replied with frosty amusement, "And what might your name be, Scout?"

"Consuela," she replied, taking great comfort from the steadiness of her voice. "And yours?"

Captain Arnol broke in, "She is an outworlder, Diplomat. Clearly she has never heard that those who represent the Hegemony pay the ultimate price of giving up their own identity."

Something in the captain's voice lifted her gaze. She

saw a clear warning in his eyes, and something more. Fear?

"A pity that the senior pilot did not include proper manners in your training, Scout," the diplomat said frostily.

But Consuela's gaze remained on Captain Arnol, as he gave his head an imperceptible shake, then from behind the diplomat lifted one open hand slightly, in caution.

The door sighed open to admit an angry gray-bearded man in white. "What is the meaning of this?"

The diplomat did not bother to look around. "And who, pray tell, are you?"

"Doctor Alvero, head of this clinic." He stepped to one side and allowed the diminutive nurse to enter the room. "I am personally responsible for the scout."

"Very well, Doctor." The head turned a fraction. "I hereby relieve you of your duties in regards to this patient."

But the doctor was not so easily cowed. "Your robes mean nothing to me, Diplomat." He almost spat out the last word. "It is your kind who have strangled our fair world. You and the Hegemony you serve have stood and watched as the pirates brought us to our knees."

The diplomat raised one hand toward his face. The robe slipped back to reveal a bright metallic band around his wrist. He spoke the single word, "Guards."

Instantly the door slid back; this time six stern-faced men cradling snub-nosed guns shouldered through, pressing Arnol and the doctor immediately toward the side wall. When the doctor protested, one of the soldiers lifted his gun and jammed it into the base of the doctor's skull. The man grew still.

The diplomat ordered, "Lift this one into the coaster."

A pair of soldiers reached for Wander, while another grasped Consuela's arms and pressed her up against the wall. She cried, "Where are you taking him?"

The one holding her asked, "What of her?"

"She is an outworlder, and of no importance whatso-ever," the diplomat sneered. "Now that the shield of this sensitive's abilities have been removed, she'll soon be scrounging for passage back to her dirty little globe."

"You won't get away with this," the doctor threatened, then groaned when the guard's nozzle jammed his face up hard against the wall.

"Ah, but I already have," the diplomat replied. He motioned for Wander's coaster to be pushed out, then ordered, "Search them, destroy the communicator, and seal the room. That should give us ample time." As he passed the captain, he paused and said, "I regret that I shall be forced to detain you with the others."

"It is an honor," Arnol replied grim-faced, "to serve the Hegemony."

"Indeed," the diplomat said dryly. "Your assistance in this matter will be duly noted." He turned and swept from the room.

Consuela felt brusque hands pat her down, then press her hard against the wall before releasing her entirely. She turned just in time to be blinded by a scorching blast from one gun, transforming the bed's headboard into a smoldering hulk. The last guard backed from the room. The door sighed shut, then glowed rosy-red as it was struck by a second bolt from the outside.

Consuela flung herself against the door, cried in frustration and pain when the unyielding portal scalded her. She turned to Captain Arnol and demanded, "Where are they taking him?"

"I did what I could," Arnol replied, his eyes on the closed door.

"Answer me," she demanded shrilly.

He turned slowly, like a man pushed beyond the limits

of his strength. "I do not know for certain. But there have been rumors . . ."

"No!" the doctor gasped. "It is too terrible to imagine that there is such a place."

"What place?" Consuela pleaded.

"A bleak world," Captain Arnol replied. "One unfit for humans, home to an ultrasecret bastion of the Hegemony."

"But why do they want Wander?" Her heart felt lanced with the sword of despair.

"That I cannot say. All I know is the Dark Couriers never relinquish what falls within their grasp." He looked at her with eyes reflecting more sorrow than she would have ever thought possible for Captain Arnol. "It is best you forget him," he said gently. "I did what I could. I saved you at least from their clutches. They thought you innocent, naive, a parasite on his powers with none of your own."

She could hold back the tears no longer. "You mean he's gone?"

"You are free. Take solace in that now in this moment of loss." Arnol turned back to the door. "For the young man, there is no hope at all."

–THREE–

The double moons graced a star-studded sky, the larger globe glowing soft and golden, the smaller a ruddy red. A broad silver river of stars stretched from horizon to horizon, with three supernovas sparkling like heavenly beacons in their midst. The evening was warm and sweet scented, and the breeze was mild. Below the balcony where she stood, a night bird sang a plaintive melody, a sound unlike anything she had ever heard before.

Consuela had never known the meaning of loneliness until that moment.

Soft movement heralded the arrival of another. "Are you all right, Scout Consuela?"

"How could I be," she softly replied, not turning around, "when I don't even know where I am?"

"You are on Avanti," the pert little nurse replied simply. Her name was Adriana, and she had attached herself firmly to Consuela's side.

When the hospital door had been forced open, the news of Wander's disappearance had raced through the staff and out into the city. Within minutes an official convoy had arrived, led by a stately matron who said she represented the chancellor, who was offering Consuela a place within the official guest house. Urged on by all, including Captain Arnol, and too confused to think clearly for herself, Consuela had accepted.

On the way through a city she scarcely saw, Adriana reported that the spaceport confirmed that the Hegemony vessel had blasted off against express orders and for an unknown destination. Consuela had allowed herself to be led into a spacious apartment, half heard the matron's assurances that she was utterly safe here, closed the bedroom door, and cried herself to sleep.

A gentle hand on her arm brought the night back into focus. "I know it is hard," Adriana told her. "But life must go on, yes? And you have an audience with the chancellor in an hour."

"I can't," Consuela said simply.

"You must." For once the nurse's gay chatter was absent. "The chancellor rules our land on behalf of the Three Planets Council. His requests are commands, and he has said that he will see you this night."

Adriana took her hand and led her back into the large bedchamber. "Look. I have laid out your scout robes."

Consuela's heart tolled the passing moments with the hollow note of a cracked bell. "What am I supposed to say to him?"

"Nothing, if you wish." Her voice remained gentle but firm. "He knows of your loss, as does all Avanti. But meet him you will. Who knows, perhaps he can help you."

A faint tug of interest lifted her gaze. "Help me do what?"

"Do whatever you must." Dark eyes met hers with shared sorrow. "At times like this, even the slenderest of hopes can offer a reason for life, no?"

When they departed an hour later, the night embraced

their passage with a warm, perfumed breeze. Because the evening was so pleasant, they traveled by open floater. To Consuela, it appeared to be nothing more than a slab of illuminated sidewalk. Adriana led her toward the white square framed by soft light. They stepped on board, and instantly polished railings rose to surround them. Adriana leaned down and spoke the words, "Palace, main entrance." Instantly the floater lifted and started away.

The floater traveled smoothly and silently at just over treetop level, taking them toward the grandest building on the horizon, surrounded as it was by a brilliant ring of light. From every peak and turret flew great flags, which appeared to shimmer with their own illumination.

Something at the corner of her vision caused her to turn around. "We're being followed."

"Guards," Adriana replied, not bothering to look. "They will be with you everywhere. It is necessary until we are sure the Hegemony takes no interest in you."

"We?" Consuela looked at her escort. "Just who are you, anyway?"

"I am a nurse," Adriana replied. "But I also serve the Three Planets and the ruling Council."

"Serve who?"

But further explanations were cut short by a brilliant shaft of light shifting around and pinpointing them. Momentarily blinded, Consuela raised her hand to shield her eyes and heard an enormous roar of noise rise up from the ground below. "What is that?"

"As I said," Adriana replied simply. "All Avanti knows."

Her eyes adjusted to the glare, Consuela leaned over and risked a glance as their floater began settling downward. Stretching out in three directions as far as she could see was a great mass of screaming, shouting, waving people. All with faces upturned. All looking at her.

At *her*.

The floater settled into a tiny island of calm. Great gold-embossed gates rose up behind them, while in front, uniformed soldiers cordoned off the crowd. A trio of larger floaters settled down alongside and in front of theirs, and a dozen stiff-faced guards joined those already flanking the crowd.

Consuela allowed Adriana to guide her off their own floater, but she could not take her eyes from the people. A forest of arms reached over the soldiers, all accompanied by faces shouting and laughing and crying. For *her*.

Consuela offered them a timid wave, and the noise became even more fervid.

Adriana touched her arm, and she turned as a cortege of guards in sharply creased uniforms passed through the open palace gates, flanking a pair of elderly statesmen in flowing robes. The guards formed a tall helmeted wall on either side of her as the statesmen approached and bowed. Because the crowd's noise overwhelmed them all, they simply motioned for her to take a station between them as they turned back toward the palace.

Only when Consuela had taken a half-dozen steps did she realize that Adriana was no longer with her. She turned back to see her newfound friend smile from her place by the floater and motion Consuela onward.

Reluctantly she turned back and allowed herself to be guided up broad steps surrounded by yet more guards, through the tallest doors she had ever seen, up a long sweeping set of broad inner stairs, through more doors, and into a vast hallway whose painted ceiling seemed truly to be as high as the sky itself. The statesmen introduced themselves with another pair of sweeping bows, then turned and began introducing her to an endless line of people. The men were groomed and polished, the women wore a spectacular array of colors and jewels. All the faces were smiling, all the people eager. To meet *her*.

Consuela allowed her hand to be taken by each person in turn, forgetting the names and titles as soon as they were spoken, scarcely seeing the faces as belonging to individuals at all. The entire scene was too overwhelming, especially coming as it did so swiftly upon the heels of all the other shocks.

Then her attention was caught and held by a tall young man who stood at the line's very end. Consuela stopped so suddenly that the statesman following bumped into her. She did not feel it.

The man wore pilot's robes.

He made a deep and sweeping bow, the gesture adding to the majesty of his looks and his robes. "Pilot Dunlevy at your service, noble sister Scout. I am on temporary assignment to Avanti's main spaceport. Might I have the honor of accompanying you?"

The pair of statesmen began an officious protest, but Consuela cut them off by offering her arm and replying, "Gladly."

He moved in as close as decorum allowed and spoke in a voice meant for her ears alone. "We have a good deal in common, you and I," he told her. "I too studied under Senior Pilot Grimson, and since then have been working on an outworld. Where is your home?"

"Baltimore," she said faintly. She glanced up at his face, guessed his age in the late twenties. A tall and striking man. If she were not suffering so from the pain of loss, she would even have called him handsome.

He shook his head in bewilderment. "Never have I heard of that one, but perhaps I know it by another name. No matter. Avanti was my birthplace, and my first allegiance is here. What has happened to this world and her sister planets is a disgrace." His voice grew heated as he leaned even closer. "I must warn you, sister Scout, there are Hegemony spies everywhere. It is for this reason that I chose to approach you here."

Something in his voice clutched at her. "You have news?"

"Move along, lest we draw unwanted ears," he said, and forced a smile to his face. "Can you laugh for the people?"

"No."

"Smile then. Not all the eyes upon us are here in this room, nor are all you see your friends."

Consuela made do with a thin grimace. "Tell me."

"The chancellor himself asked me home. He knows my family, and through them asked me to vacation here and see if I could help in solving the mystery."

"What—"

He gestured her to silence. "Later. We have only until those doors up ahead. I was at the spaceport when the Hegemony vessel blasted in earlier today, unannounced and uninvited. I was there too when it left."

Consuela stopped and wheeled about. "You saw where it went?"

"The quadrant only." His face stretched taut in a smile that cost him much. "Alas, I am not a Talent." He backed away and into another sweeping bow, then raised his voice so that it carried to those who sought to cluster close. "An honor to make your acquaintance, sister Scout. Perhaps you would do me the esteem of joining me at the spaceport tomorrow."

"Of course," Consuela replied, trying hard to match his formal manner.

"Excellent. Shall we say at noon?"

–FOUR–

The chancellor's inner sanctum was not as grand as the formal hall, but in its own way just as elegant. The great oval-shaped chamber was surrounded by tall pillars supporting a domed ceiling colored like a sky at dawn. The carpet was embossed with what appeared to be three planets forming a triangle, with a pair of brilliant stars gleaming from their epicenter.

"Scout Consuela, what an honor and a privilege." The chancellor was a gray-haired gentleman who required neither height nor girth to grant him the stature of power. He wore his office like an invisible mantle, and authority shone from his clear gray eyes. He turned to the hovering statesmen and said, "Thank you, gentlemen, that will be all."

Clearly this was not what they expected or desired. "But sire—"

The chancellor needed only to raise his head a fraction and glance in their direction for both to bow and scurry from the room. When the great portals were closed behind them, he said with quiet solemnity, "All Avanti grieves with you at this time of loss and sorrow."

Consuela found herself losing control beneath the power of this man's genuine kindness. She stiffened her chin to stop it from quivering, took a long breath, managed, "Thank you."

He took note of her struggle for control with a single nod of approval. "Come over here and sit down. We shall not have much time to speak alone today. Avanti clamors for you. Later, perhaps, but not now. So you will excuse me if I do away with protocol."

Consuela allowed herself to be guided into a brocade chair with gold-embossed arms and made do with a nod.

"The good Captain Arnol tells me that you are a practical and level-headed young woman. And that you are indeed a Talent. Is all this true?"

His abrupt manner startled her into an equally direct reply. "Yes."

"Then I will come right to the point. We have long suspected that the Hegemony monitors the reaches available only to you Talents. How, we do not know, but we suspect that they must have amplifiers, the powers of which we cannot begin to imagine. Amplifiers so enormously potent that they can reach to the very borders of the empire. And they use these to constantly search out the sensitives who might have escaped them."

"But why?"

"I was hoping you could tell me that for yourself."

Consuela inspected the strong stalwart face and decided that here was a man she could trust. "I did not even know I was a sensitive myself until a few weeks ago. To be honest, I still find it a little hard to believe."

"I am sorry to hear that." The chancellor showed genuine disappointment. "Well, I suppose I should take comfort in the fact that your freshness no doubt explains how you managed to escape their clutches. Nonetheless, I am disappointed not to have an opportunity to have some of the mysteries encircling the Hegemony's use of Talents resolved."

"I don't understand," Consuela said. "Aren't you a member of the Hegemony?"

"In word and on paper, yes," the chancellor replied, his face settling into grim lines. "But in truth, less and less with each passing day. You see, we who make up the Three Planets were growing daily in power. Up until ten years ago, we pledged our unswerving loyalty to the Hegemony, and did so willingly. Still, they did not trust us. We were rich and growing richer. Other nearby star systems began forging stronger and stronger links, turning to us in times of trouble, rather than to the Hegemony. Our industrial might was unsurpassed. Our academies turned out the finest minds in the empire. Then everything changed."

Then he stopped and looked at her, as though willing her to find the answer for herself. It dawned with blinding suddenness. "Pirates."

"Precisely," the chancellor said approvingly. "Whether or not the Hegemony is behind their stranglehold, we cannot be sure. But what we do know is that help has not been forthcoming. Furthermore, on one point the Hegemony's rule is unbending; no single system is permitted to arm itself beyond what is required to police its own internal borders. We have long felt that the local Emissary has orders to do nothing but stand aside and watch us suffer."

"It has been hard for you," Consuela observed, for the moment drawn beyond her own loss by the chancellor's gravity.

"Worse than that, my dear. We are a trading system. It is another reason why the Hegemony is jealous of our wealth, for we compete directly with their own traders. Or did. Now we are cut off. And as a result, the Three Planets are slowly dying."

Consuela studied the man's open gaze, realized that someone of his power and position would take the time to speak with her only if something important was required from her. Despite the fog of her heavy heart, she understood what he was driving at. "Your goals and mine are the same."

"I am most glad to learn that Captain Arnol's assessment of you is correct," the chancellor approved. "You want to find your special man. We want to know where the Hegemony has taken him. And why."

My special man. Just hearing the words warmed the night with hope. "I met a pilot outside. He says he may have found something."

"Yes, I have read the pilot's report." Clearly the chancellor was less than optimistic. "I know Dunlevy's family. They are good people. It was a long shot, requesting that he return. But to identify a possible segment of the empire, which contains several hundred systems . . ." He gave a grim shrug. "In any case, tell him that anything he requires, anything at all, shall be placed instantly at his disposal. And yours.'"

"Thank you," she said, moved despite her own heartache by the man's noble strength.

"Adriana knows how to reach me at any time of night or day. If you find something of even possible use in our quest, do not hesitate to contact me."

A quest. *Our* quest. "You know my nurse?"

"Adriana is both my own niece and one of a very special breed," he replied, rising to his feet. "Above all else, she is a patriot. Come, my dear. We must hold further talk for another time and give the people their due."

He led her across the chamber, pulled back heavy

drapes embossed with the emblem of what appeared to be two suns, and revealed a tall glass portal. It was only as Consuela followed him through the doorway that she realized he walked with a slight stoop, as though weighed down by the invisible burdens he carried.

The balcony had been prepared for them, and was draped in bunting and flowers. Consuela stepped outside, waited while her eyes adjusted to the spotlights' glare, and felt the waves of sound crash over her.

The chancellor permitted the tumult to continue for a short time, then raised his hands high and waited until the hubbub had eased. "My friends and fellow citizens of Avanti," he declared, his voice amplified by a hidden microphone so that it rang out through the surrounding night. "It is with great joy that I stand here and proclaim with you the first sign of hope that we have known in ten long years."

The rejoicing below carried a sense of renewed hope, so strong that even Consuela's wounded heart knew a moment's relief. So it was with a smile that she met the chancellor when he turned toward her, and from an embossed wooden case brought out a shining gold medallion hung from a ribbon of rainbow colors.

"Scout Consuela," the chancellor said, his voice booming through the unseen speakers, "while you lay, still suffering from the wounds received in our defense, your shipmates have already been so honored. Now it is your turn to be declared a Knight of the Three Planet Realm. All Avanti is in your debt."

Consuela bowed her head and allowed the chancellor to place the ribbon around her neck. She then turned to the crowd and raised the medal toward them, the smile still coming easy. When the clamor had run its course, once more the chancellor raised his hands for silence. He then lifted a second slender box high over his head. "One other should also be standing here, sharing in the glory, and receiving his well-earned acclaim."

The words were carried out and echoed back over a suddenly silent crowd. Their abrupt stillness caused her to realize what enormous risk the chancellor was taking, speaking thus in public. It was an unequivocal and direct challenge to the Hegemony.

"Scout Consuela," the chancellor went on, turning back and extending to her the box. "I charge you with delivering this tribute, along with our heartfelt thanks, for the part that Scout Wander played in our triumph."

Consuela accepted the box, turned to the crowd, lifted the box over her own head, and spoke for the first time since walking out on the balcony. "I will deliver this," she said. "You have my word."

– FIVE –

The Avanti spaceport was a massive affair, made enormously depressing by its emptiness.

Consuela arrived well before noontime, unable to wait any longer to learn what she could of Wander's destination. Nothing could have prepared her for what she found.

As usual, she was accompanied on the floater by Adriana, and surrounded by a sweeping phalanx of guards. The day was overcast, the air so heavy with approaching rain that it felt thick in her lungs. Thankfully, the trip was not long, as the spaceport lay on the same side of the capital city as the consular palace.

The port was void of activity. She could see that long before they landed. The vast space set aside for ground transport was almost empty. And there were no people at all. No movement around the empty thruster pads or the long line of colossal warehouses or the terminal itself. None.

Throughout the entire time of their approach, a single ship glided in, small and scarred and clearly intended for little more than lunar transport. Beyond the terminal, Consuela saw how weeds were pushing up between segments of the cracked and pitted concrete surrounding the launch pads.

"Ten years," Adriana said quietly as the floater came to a halt. "Ten years we have watched as our world has slowly been strangled."

Consuela peered through the sweeping expanse of glass and saw only vast, empty spaces adorned with chrome and polished surfaces and gleaming artwork. But no people. "This is terrible."

"Before, it was said that Avanti lived and died by trade. Can the Hegemony truly not see what the pirates are doing here? I and most others think not." She motioned toward the door. "Come, let us enter."

The main hall was even grander than the spaceport where she had met Wander. The walls were rose-colored stone streaked with what appeared to be real gold. They changed colors dramatically as the sun finally emerged from behind the heavily overcast sky. Consuela looked up through the polarized ceiling glass and gasped.

Not sun. *Suns.* Plural. Two of them.

One great and orangish red, the other smaller and bright as an arc-lamp even through the glass. She shielded her eyes, saw how twin strands of brilliant power flowed from the top and the bottom of the larger sun, like ribbons of light tying the suns together. "Incredible," she breathed.

"Careful," hissed Adriana at her side, and from the corner of her eye she saw the guards stiffen to full alert. "The Emissary."

Consuela lowered her head, saw an obese figure in flowing multicolored robes approaching them. He was flanked by stern-faced warriors with weapons at the ready. Despite the evident danger, she was far from frightened. Her growing anger left no room for fear. Besides, the fat man looked as though he were dressed in an over-bright bathrobe.

"Well, well, what have we here?" The silken voice carried undercurrents of dedicated cruelty. "If it is not the glorious scout. Or perhaps I should say, Knight Scout. Ah, but has she neglected to wear her well-earned medal of honor?"

Consuela squeezed down tight on her fury, focusing it with the precision of aiming down a rifle barrel. She walked straight up to him, so close that he not only stopped talking but jerked back a half step in surprise. Her eyes only inches from his, she said, "I want to know where you've taken him."

Eyes slit down in calculated coldness. "Missing our little Talent, are we? How sad."

"What you and your people did to Wander was as evil as what you're doing to this planet."

He drew himself up and back, then gathered his dignity with a sweeping motion of his robes. "You would be well advised to watch your brazen tongue."

Her gaze did not budge. "I'm not afraid of you."

"Ah, but you should be." He started to say more but glanced uneasily at the guards, tensed and close at hand. Eyes hard as marbles turned back to her, and with a little mock bow he said, "We shall meet again, Scout. Of that I am certain."

Only when the outer doors had sighed shut behind him did Adriana murmur, "I am not sure that was wise."

"I don't care," Consuela replied stubbornly. "I'm in no mood to play games with a worm."

"He is that," Adriana agreed. "Come, the pilot is waiting."

Like everything else about the spaceport, the control tower was twice the size of the only other she had seen. There were two half-moon control-mounds, set at an angle to each other so that they faced out over two separate collections of thruster pads. All this only made the emptiness even more aching. There were a total of four people on duty when they entered, all of them gathered in a cluster around the Watch Commandant's station and ignoring the barren fields outside.

Pilot Dunlevy detached himself from the little group, walked over, spoke a greeting to Adriana, then bowed to Consuela. "It is indeed an honor to meet you again," he said formally. "All the staff here are friends, and are to be trusted. Before we go on, allow me to say for all of us here how sorry we are over your distress. I hope you believe me when I say that this is truly all Avanti's loss."

The words and the genuine concern behind them were almost enough to shatter her fragile hold on control. Mentally Consuela pushed aside his words, drew herself back from the brink, and said, "What I'd like to know is how they got in so easily. If you were so concerned about their plotting against you, you'd have thought to put a couple of guards out there."

"The hospital was *surrounded* with guards," he responded defensively. "Top to bottom, the place was *sealed*. But they were warned to bar entry to strangers, not to officers of the Hegemony. Even the toughest of guards would think twice about questioning a diplomat."

"So they just walked in," Consuela said, sorrow welling up once again. "And took him."

"Never for a moment did we think they would operate so openly," Dunlevy said. "It is a first, and demonstrates just how desperately they wanted him."

"But *why?*"

"I wish I knew," Dunlevy replied grimly.

His helpless frustration pushed at her, forcing her once more toward the edge. Her eyes brimmed over with the same burning loss which seared her chest, and she had to turn away.

Dunlevy noticed her distress and changed the subject with, "You outworlders don't have much time for us from the privileged classes, do you?"

She made a rapid swipe of her eyes and hedged, "I'm not sure I know what you mean."

"Yes, you do," he replied. "Did you ever stop to wonder why we were given such preferential treatment? It's because we're more easily controlled."

"By the Hegemony?"

"Training young people to be pilots is a two-edged sword," he went on, his voice cutting like raw acid. "They need us in order to guide their ships and hold their empire together. But handing such power to young people who have not come up through the proper Hegemony ranks is dangerous business. So they cull those they can from the landed gentry, families with the most to lose. Their hope is that the parents of these young people will have instilled in them a sense of loyalty to the Hegemony. But if not, then these are people whose families they can get to easily and hold for ransom or worse."

She inspected his finely chiseled features, asked, "Are they doing this to you?"

"Not yet," he answered. "After an absence of almost three years, I have every right to come and visit my family. But the emissary was not here to see you. Not just, anyway."

"What did he say?"

"Nothing much." Bitterness stretched his features taut. "Just asked about my sister's health. She requires a medicine that isn't available on Avanti. Without it she wouldn't last a week."

"He would do that?"

Dunlevy's eyes remained on the control tower's closed portals. "He knew and I knew. The message was clear. I must do the Hegemony's bidding or my family suffers."

Consuela took a long mental step back, then said in a subdued voice, "I can't ask you to take that risk."

He looked down at her. "What are you talking about?"

"Trading your sister's life for information about where Wander might have been taken," she replied. "I couldn't live with myself."

For the first time since they had met, Dunlevy showed genuine humor. "If they even suspected I had followed the diplomat ship's departure, you would be talking to a little pile of ashes."

Hope sprang anew in her heart. "Then you'll help me?"

"You still don't realize how big this matter really is, do you?" He turned and took the stairs to the pilot's chair in long strides. "Come up here and hook up."

Consuela followed him slowly, slid into the chair next to his, looked at the headset he jammed into her hands, and hesitated. Then it hit her. She was sitting unshielded in a control tower and was hearing no voices. She looked out through the main windows at the empty vista before her and realized for the first time just how cut off Avanti really had become.

She handed back the headset. "I can't use this."

He looked up distractedly from his adjusting of the amp controls. "Why, what's the matter?"

She studied his face a moment, then replied, "I think it's time I trusted you."

His hands became utterly still. "What are you talking about?"

"If I plugged myself into that amp with this," she said, indicating the headset in his hands, "you'd have a scream-ing idiot on your hands in no time flat. I know. I've done it."

The blaze of triumph came and went with the speed of

a lightning strike. He leaned forward and hissed, "You're a Talent?"

"Just so you understand, let me tell you exactly what I am," Consuela replied. "I am somebody with exactly zero training on watch, and with precisely one space trip under her belt."

Quietly she outlined her days at the port, leaving out her unexplained arrival, but little else. How she collapsed at the onset of her first class, and had scarcely recovered when Senior Pilot Grimson had shuttled her up to the tower, reacted just as Dunlevy did when she complained of voices—

"Without amplification?" Dunlevy's agitation was so great he could scarcely hold himself in the chair. "You heard the control tower's communications even when you weren't hooked in?"

"Not only that," she said, and told him of watching the ship's departure with Wander, feeling time slow with the countdown, until she felt connected to the moment beyond time when the gravity shield was released and the ship departed.

With that, Dunlevy appeared to stop breathing. He swiveled around to face out over the empty field and stared at nothing for the longest time before whispering, "I had heard rumors. We all did. That there really were sensitives whose abilities broke all the known boundaries. I thought they were legends."

"There's more." Consuela waited until he had swung back around, then told him of the pilot's sudden appearance, and how they had been rushed into Captain Arnol's ship. How on the voyage she and Wander had been simply experimenting with the mind-amp controls, trying to extend their senses out as far as they could without losing shipboard contact, when they had found the shadowlanes.

"Arnol mentioned this," Dunlevy murmured. "I had trouble believing him, though." He inspected her. "Another legend come to life."

"You have spoken with the captain? When?"

Dunlevy waved it aside. "Finish your story, then we will move on to other things."

"There isn't much else. We tracked down each shadow-lane as we approached, and on the third we found the pirate ship. Captain Arnol planned to attack first, but I guess they got in one shot, because the next thing I knew I was here in the hospital."

Dunlevy sat in silence a moment longer. "Two Talents in the same class, and a diplomat's ship suddenly appearing out of nowhere," he said to himself. "No wonder Grimson panicked."

"How is he?"

"Worried, of that I am sure." He raised himself with difficulty from his reverie. "He should be made aware of what has transpired. Would you like to speak with him?"

Suddenly Consuela found herself missing the stern-visaged teacher. "Very much."

A second hint of genuine humor surfaced. "I understand your sentiments perfectly. He is a fright to study under, but whenever I am faced with the unsolvable, I try to do what I think he would expect of me." Dunlevy bounded to his feet. "But first we shall find you a damped headset, second I shall show you the quadrant where they took your Wander, and then you will see what our dear Master Grimson has to say for himself."

He left and returned with impatient swiftness. He plugged her in, then sat and watched her adjust the headset's damping effect. He leaned over, read the dial, and sat back with a bemused expression. "You can truly detect the amplifier's power at this stage?"

"Any more and I'd be climbing the walls," Consuela replied.

"Then perhaps there is hope after all." Agitation sped his movements as he bent over the amp's controls and said, "Just relax and follow my lead."

"I don't—" Consuela stopped as her focus was drawn first out to the nearest thruster shield, then out and up. And up. And farther still. "Oh my."

"Relax," he said, his hands busy, powering them together farther and farther away. "Stay alert."

Here was the power of a pilot on watch, she realized. Here was what her lack of training kept her from both doing and fully understanding. Not simply communicating with oncoming and outgoing ships. Not simply sending messages and directions out across the vastness of space. But *connecting* with space. Reaching through the limits, and beyond, yet all the while resting steady and in control there in the tower.

Consuela felt herself sitting and breathing and feeling her racing heart, yet at the same time found herself being guided farther and farther out through the heavens, remaining steady only because she was fastened firmly to Dunlevy. Farther and faster she moved, and knew that here was one skilled and trained and truly in control.

"There," he finally announced, the whispered word resounding out in the stars where her mind was reaching. "This is as far as I managed to follow. I do not know if they were cloaked in some way, or simply passed beyond my ability to track them. But this is the quadrant where they were headed."

Even under his steady direction, all she saw was a limitless field of unknown space. She felt as much as saw him draw barriers that limited the range to a sort of distended cone, yet even here the expanse was enormous. "So many stars," she whispered.

"Two hundred and forty inhabited systems," he agreed dismally. "Not to mention twice as many that are not yet charted, or have no known planets, or simply are not thought to hold anything of worth."

With a sweep of his hand he drew them back, the instant of her return so shocking she was forced away from the seeming hopelessness of their challenge, and back into the relatively safe confines of the tower. Consuela took a breath, said, "That was incredible."

"The tricks of our craft," he said deferentially. "Had it been you up here, perhaps we could have identified precisely where they landed."

"Had it been me up here," Consuela replied, "I would never have left the field."

If he realized she was paying him a compliment, he did not show it. "And now to see if our dear Senior Pilot Grimson is available."

Again there was the sweeping outward, this time focused into a beam that followed a tightly controlled path. Consuela allowed herself to be swept along. She recognized even more clearly that having extra talent did not in any way make up for a lack of training.

There was a sense of planetary approach, then the call from Dunlevy, *This is Avanti Spaceport, Watch Communicator calling with a message for Senior Pilot Grimson.*

He is off watch, came the droned reply. *Report and I will pass on.*

Negative. This message carries priority one, code red.

You had better be right, Communicator, came the laconic reply. *Grimson hates to be disturbed when he is teaching.*

This is urgent, Dunlevy stubbornly repeated. *I take full responsibility.*

Hold on, came the response, and the contact ended.

Consuela waited with the patience of one who could scarcely comprehend what she was sensing. There she sat, safe and calm in a chair which molded to her in a comfortable support, looking out through tower windows at the broad expanse of empty field. And yet at the same time she was suspended in space, in contact with a world so distant she could not have found it on the clearest of nights, even if she had known where to look. Aware of the world about her, and still able to see out and through the endless night of space.

Grimson here, came the familiar icy voice. *This had better be good.*

Dunlevy reporting, Senior Pilot. I have a friend of yours here with me.

Consuela found it possible to extend her thoughts better if she whispered softly. *Hello, Senior Pilot.*

Instantly came the sharp response, *Hold!* Then nothing.

Consuela drew back and looked toward Dunlevy, but he remained motionless, save for the lifting of a single finger. Wait.

A few moments later Grimson returned. *All right. This is as secure a channel as I can arrange on short notice. What news?*

Very little positive to report, Senior Pilot. Swiftly Dunlevy sketched all that he knew—starting with their discovery of the shadowlane and the pirates, ending with Wander's forced disappearance. Dunlevy spoke with the terse compactness of one accustomed to giving official reports. When he finished he simply stopped and waited.

I knew it was too good to be true when the diplomatic vessel departed so swiftly, Grimson said finally. *They were headed your way.*

Are you under suspicion?

If so, it is nothing more than that. For the moment, in any case. My records show clearly that a training flight was arranged for two gifted students. Nothing more, nothing less. What they may surmise, when given time to reconsider, is anyone's guess.

Consuela could stand it no longer. *Where have they taken Wander?*

That I cannot tell you. A trace of sympathy crept into Grimson's disciplined calm. *It is one of the Hegemony's most closely guarded secrets.*

If it exists at all, Dunlevy added.

Of that I have no doubt whatsoever, Grimson responded. *Wander is not the first Talent I have lost to the diplomats.*

Of course, Dunlevy said slowly. *That was why you took immediate steps to send this pair away.*

Of no avail, I fear, Grimson said. *For Wander, at least.*

But Consuela refused to accept the note of hopelessness, even for a moment. *Dunlevy watched the diplomat's ship depart.*

A keenness surged across immeasurable distances. *You tracked the ship?*

To the quadrant only.

Tell me.

Vector Nine.

So far. The senior pilot was silent. *There was once a Hegemony battle station out that way. Before my time, but my own teacher had apprenticed there as a newly released scout. A terrible place, he said, one so horrible not even battle-scarred troops could stand it for long. Then the empire's borders were extended outward, and to everyone's relief the station was moved.*

And the planet?

Abandoned. Grimson hesitated, then offered, *Or so they say.*

This could be it. Dunlevy's own excitement remained barely under control. *You have the coordinates?*

Somewhere. I shall scour the records this very day.

This is news the chancellor must hear, Dunlevy said. *Does the planet have a name?*

Indeed, Grimson answered. *Taken from a time beyond time, or so legend has it. They called it Citadel.*

– Six –

Rick found himself growing enormously bored.

He would have never imagined such a thing possible. But he missed the stringent challenge of combat, of being tested to his limits and beyond.

No question about it. Having a life of wine, women, and song grew stale faster than he would have ever thought possible.

News of their having captured a pirate vessel arrived before their ship did, as Arnol's first report had been broadcast all over the planet Avanti. They landed at a spaceport full not of ships, but of people. Rick would never forget that sight as long as he lived, a mass of people stretching out in every direction as far as he could see.

It was only with time that he and the others began to understand why they had received the greeting they did. How for ten years the world had begged and pleaded with the Hegemony for assistance against the pirates, and how the Hegemony had replied time after time, "What pirates are these?" For the Hegemony's official position was that, yes, of course, there were the occasional villains. But as to an organized band waging war for profit in space? Inside the Hegemony's borders? Absolute nonsense. And since nobody had ever encountered pirates and lived to tell the tale, all they had to go on were snatches of cut-off conversations and rumors of outworld slavers fattened with the product of pirate attacks.

But now they had captured a pirate vessel. Intact, with crew alive. And done not by a Hegemony battle fleet, bristling with men and weaponry. No, by a single trader traversing the Hegemony lightways, alone and outfitted with a grand total of four weapons officers and two trainee scouts.

Truly this was the stuff of legends.

Rick found himself singled out for special attention. For when the full account was heard, the world learned that it was he who had saved the ship by overcoming the effects of the stunner blast and firing off three well-aimed bolts of his own. The chancellor himself mentioned his actions at the reception honoring the crew before awarding him the same knighthood medal that they all now wore.

Things started heating up that same night.

Scarcely had he recovered from the spotlight's shock when the first women approached him. Their manners and their speech left no room for doubt. And it was not just one. Lady after highborn lady had drawn near and made him offers that had set his ears aflame and left him unsure whether to laugh out loud or pinch himself to make sure he was not dreaming. By the end of the night he felt ten feet tall and loaded for bear.

But to his utter amazement, within a week the adoring fans who followed them everywhere, the adulation and everything that accompanied it, all began to fade. Rick found himself yearning for the relative simplicity of space.

That very morning the captain noticed the change, and approved. At breakfast he had observed Rick seated glumly in the kitchen of their palatial quarters and remarked, "There's hope for you yet, Lieutenant."

"Captain?"

"I have accepted a somewhat irregular request from the local Chancellor, one that will have to remain confidential for a while longer. To be perfectly honest, I know little of the details myself. But I have decided to trust the chancellor and respect his need for secrecy. I'm sending the ship onward under the command of my number two." Arnol inspected him over the rim of his coffee mug, then said, "I've decided to keep you here with me."

Rick scrambled to his feet. "If it's all the same with you, Captain, I'd rather get back into action."

"I see that you would," Arnol said approvingly. "That is precisely why I have decided to hold you over. You and Guns will be my weapons contingent."

"For what, Captain? We won't have a ship."

"At the moment. Things are brewing beyond the horizon, that's all I can tell you." Arnol set down his cup. "I have a meeting this morning with the chancellor. Perhaps there will be more to report later on."

Glumly Rick had spent the morning watching most of his crewmates pack up and set off. No matter what the captain said, he genuinely wished to be among them. And Guns was no help. The grizzled weapons officer had not stirred in almost two days. He had the ability to store up sleep and food as a camel did water.

"Ten-hut!"

Rick bounced to his feet, then realized the sound had come from far down the corridor. The captain. Arnol must have returned. Swiftly he donned his uniform and scurried to the front gallery.

"Ah, Lieutenant, good. Is Guns with us?"

Rick found himself unable to respond, his attention

captured by the entourage accompanying Captain Arnol. The chancellor was there, along with a pair of statesmen, plus a tall man in pilot's robes, plus guards. Lots of guards.

And Consuela.

She entered the room and brought a shadow with her. Although she held herself erect, it was with effort. Her features looked hollowed out by some pain so deep he could only guess at it. It was strange, seeing so young a face locked in such grief. Yet it was real. He only had to look at her eyes to know that she was truly in agony over Wander's kidnapping.

They had all heard of it, of course. Even Guns, the harshest critic of the pilot class, now classified these two as a breed apart. When they had heard how the diplomat had broken into the hospital, kidnapped Wander only moments after he had been revived, blasted the room's controls, sealed them all inside, then made their escape with warriors guarding their exit, they had all wanted vengeance. It was a matter of pride for them, that and the desire to hunt down more pirates—and for that they needed Wander's abilities.

But this was something entirely different. Rick stared at Consuela, and somehow the sorrow etched on her face made the women and the celebrations and his experiences of the past few days seem even more hollow.

"Lieutenant."

He snapped to alert. "Captain, Guns is still asleep, far as I know."

"What about the others?"

"Tucker is about. I believe that's it."

"Go and rouse Guns, will you. Tell him to get out here and be swift about it."

But evidently the weapons officer's internal tracking system worked even in sleep, for he was already up and dressing when Rick arrived. "What's up, mate?"

"Captain wants you on the bounce."

"Let's be at it, then." As they passed back down the corridor, Guns asked, "Any idea what's behind this?"

Rick shook his head. "But the chancellor's here. And Consuela."

To his surprise, Guns actually brightened at the news. "Lass is up and about, is she? Good. That's real good."

They entered the vast main gallery to find Chief Petty Officer Tucker seated among the gathering, which had requisitioned the chamber's far side and now been cordoned off by alert guards. Tucker, a tall burly officer, was another of the crew ordered to remain behind when the ship had blasted off that very day. His response had blistered paint at thirty paces, but only after the captain had departed.

Now he wore a different expression entirely. He sat in formal alertness, no surprise given the presence of both the captain and the chancellor, not to mention the other silent statesmen. But there was no disguising the battle gleam in his eyes.

"Ah, Guns, good of you to join us. You remember the chancellor."

"Aye, Captain." He saluted the chancellor, then turned and gave a formal bow of greeting toward Consuela. "Knew you were too tough to keep down for long. Nice to see you up and about."

Consuela managed a fleeting smile. "Hello, Guns."

"No need to worry, lass. We're going to bring the boyo back," Guns promised quietly. "You can take my very oath on that one."

"A worthy sentiment," the chancellor stated.

Consuela was forced to turn away for a moment, but not before the raw edge of her grief was exposed. Tucker reached over from the chair beside hers and enveloped her hands in one hairy paw. She took a breath, gave him a look of genuine gratitude.

"I need not tell anyone," the chancellor began, "that anything discussed at this or any other time is to be held in strictest confidence. Your dwelling is as safe as anywhere on this planet, but outside these portals you may assume to find Hegemony spies lurking everywhere." He scanned the group to ensure that his message had struck home, then nodded toward the captain.

"Now that we are all present," Captain Arnol said, "allow me to introduce Pilot Dunlevy, a man claimed as friend by our scout and vouched for by the chancellor. He has news that may interest us."

Dunlevy leaned forward and swiftly sketched his tracking of the Hegemony vessel and then his contact with Senior Pilot Grimson. "I have just come from communicating with him. To his utter astonishment, Grimson could find no record anywhere of a planet known as Citadel."

The chancellor tensed. "This is true?"

"I know this Grimson," Captain Arnol interjected. "Both by reputation and in person. He is a man of unquestioned integrity. If he says something, you can rest assured it is true."

"Grimson was up the entire night," Dunlevy went on, "checking through all records held by the spaceport library, going back to the original Hegemony mapping ships. Because they are a scout training station, they also hold numerous duplicates of master archive files. He found nothing. And yet the more he searched, the more he became convinced his own teacher had specifically told him of this world."

There was a moment of stunned silence, then the statesman seated beside the chancellor breathed, "Then we have found the target."

"Found it and lost it all in the same moment," muttered his compatriot.

"Not necessarily," responded the chancellor. "All we need to do is have a reason to go to that quadrant and make inquiries."

Tucker shifted uncomfortably in his seat. "Begging the master's pardon, but I'm afraid I've been lost somewhere out beyond the outer orbit."

The chancellor's smile came and went with fleeting swiftness. "Your pardon, Chief Petty Officer. I shall start at the beginning." He nodded toward Arnol and said, "I asked your good captain to remain behind and to hold this chosen few with him for a reason that I could not at the time explain to anyone else. First, I needed to receive permission from the Three Planet Council, which was finally granted this afternoon. It is a measure of your captain's loathing for our common enemy that he agreed to assist me, even to the point of giving up his command and perhaps his standing within the Hegemony fleet."

"I lost my allegiance to the Hegemony," Arnol replied implacably, "when I saw undeniable evidence that my command and the pirates are truly linked."

"They are indeed, as we have long suspected," the chancellor replied. "Your capture of the pirate vessel pointed clearly in this direction, and our questioning of the pirate captain has confirmed it. Despite the best efforts, I might add, of the Hegemony's emissary to pluck the pirate crew from our custody."

"Not to mention confirming location of a pirate hideout in our vicinity," a statesman added.

"Indeed." The chancellor again paused to look about the gathering, then continued, "And now, my friends, it is time to attack."

Tucker responded for them all. "Begging your pardon, sir, but with what?"

"For over a year," the chancellor replied, "a contingent of my ground forces have been working in top secret conditions preparing a response to these pirates."

"A warship." Arnol leaned forward in his seat. "Just as I had hoped."

"More than just a single warship, Captain. And in the guise of a mining vessel."

Guns cleared his throat. "Pardon, sir, but the Hegemony has not heard of this?"

"The fact that I am still here speaking with you indicates that we have managed to keep this a secret," the chancellor replied. "But at such a cost that I cannot begin to describe. We declared to all and sundry that we were building this mining vessel. We then placed our workstation in an environment so hostile that no official would care to make more than a cursory inspection. We even made public offers for its eventual sale. But of course there were no takers. We were once known throughout the empire for the quality of our wares. Now few are interested in even talking with us, for goods ordered from our factories never arrive."

The chancellor leaned back, his face etched with both determination and fatigue. "Throughout the period of this ship's assembly, all workers and their families have been isolated from outside contact. Only the most trusted of garrisons have been involved in transport of materials. You have heard me say that Hegemony spies are everywhere. Still, despite all odds, we have accomplished this task through a combination of stern discipline and strict diligence and unselfish patriotism shown by many."

Captain Arnol inquired, "What had you planned to do with this vessel?"

"Attack," the chancellor repeated. "Where, we were not

sure, but *what* we knew from the outset. If the Hegemony refused to stop the pirates, then we were going to have to try ourselves."

"In utter secrecy," the statesman added.

"This was our plan," the chancellor stated, leaning forward and lowering his voice. "We wanted to strike a blow not just against the pirates, but against the Hegemony itself. Let them know that they were not invulnerable. Nor could they continue to crush our lands without retribution."

"In utter secrecy," the statesman repeated.

"Precisely. Done in such a way that they would never know who it was behind it, not for certain. Sowing doubt among their own people. Demonstrating in the clearest way possible that if they do not govern with fairness, enemies they have made for themselves can and will strike at their very heart."

"And what better way to demonstrate this," Arnol finished for him, "than to attack pirates which the Hegemony claim do not exist, and then destroy a pirate stronghold for which there is no record."

"And rescue a man the Hegemony has kidnapped," Consuela said quietly, speaking for the first time.

The chancellor turned to her. "On you there must be placed a special burden. For the attempt to rescue Scout Wander, we ask you to promise us five years of service. Whether or not we are successful, with or without him, if we in turn give you our joint oath to do all within our power to bring him out."

"Five years," she murmured. "So long."

"We must have a network developed that protects us from pirate attack," the chancellor went on intently. "We *must*. It would be foolish to assume that one blow will be enough to ensure our safety. Only a Talent can help us by watching both lightways and shadowlanes for our transports." He stopped, then corrected himself, "Or Talents, if we are successful."

"I don't even know if it would be possible." Consuela thought a long moment, then squared her shoulders and said quietly, "But if I am able, I will stay."

Rick looked at her in astonishment. It was increcible that she would feel so deeply for the young man. Here she was committing herself to five *years* in a place that could not be any farther from her home. And for what? For somebody whom she scarcely even knew. As he watched her, he found himself growing angry. Why should she care so much for this Wander? Why did she not even bother to look at him anymore? Rick stared at her, consumed by sudden jealousy.

The chancellor turned to Captain Arnol and went on, "You have heard me describe how our own spacebound forces have been decimated. All our merchant fleet, all our trained officers and able-bodied spacemen, all gradually drained off through forced conscription. We have trained some of our ground forces in secret, but we need a captain." The chancellor looked from one to the other. "We need flight officers who will shape these soldiers into a cohesive fighting force. We need warriors who will take the battle to the enemy, and who will return to us with victory in their grasp."

Rick found Consuela standing alone in the archway separating the residence's main doors from the wrought-iron outer gate. She was shielding her face with one hand and staring up at the dual suns. "Sure is a long way from home, isn't it?"

She dropped her hand and turned around. "How have you been, Rick?"

Her solemn visage, her ethereal beauty, left him feeling uncomfortable and unsure of how to react. He gave his best grin and shrugged. "Not bad. Tired of being cooped up in these quarters."

"They've given you a palace and everything else you could ask for." Her sorrow lent her an almost regal dignity. "You're a hero. Aren't you enjoying that?"

"Sure." He felt unsettled. She had somehow grown older and wiser than he. "But it's sort of like cotton candy, all fluff and no substance."

She turned back to the sky. "I went home the other night."

"You mean, real home? Back to earth?"

She nodded. "My mother is sick."

Rick did not know how he felt about it. Home. Did he want to go back? Having the option made suddenly possible left him unsettled. "How did you do it?"

"I don't know. But I went. It was while I was still in the hospital." She looked at him. "I went to see your parents."

"You did? Why?"

"I felt as though they should know you were all right."

He felt ashamed then, without understanding why. And touched. She had done something for him, something he would never in a million years have thought of doing for her had their positions been reversed. "I bet they rolled out the old red carpet for you."

"They were horrible," she said, her voice empty of bitterness. "They didn't even invite me to sit down. They left me standing in the front hall under that huge portrait, and they grilled me."

"Yeah, that sounds like dear old Mom and Dad," Rick said. "I can just hear them now." He lowered his voice to a parody of his father's. "I cannot comprehend what would cause that boy to shame the family name like this."

"I don't recall his actually calling you a boy," Consuela said. "But you have the rest of it pretty straight."

"Incredible," Rick said bitterly. "They make me feel like some employee brought in to make them look good."

The sympathy and compassion that showed in her eyes came straight from the heart. "Poor Rick," she said quietly. "To have so much, and yet to suffer from the same loneliness as me."

Her words moved him deeply, as though she had reached out and touched his heart with her own. He started to speak, to tell her that he was there, to ask her to remember this if Wander was not found. But before he could open his mouth, another set of footsteps approached, and he heard Captain Arnol say, "Ah, Scout, excellent. Would you care to change quarters and join the rest of my crew?"

To Rick's relief and pleasure, Consuela read Arnol's words as the polite order that they were. "That would be fine, Captain."

"Excellent. Like to have all my personnel under one roof when there's a concern over security." He looked back at the vast palace set in its own grounds, said, "I imagine we can find quarters for the scout here, don't you, Lieutenant?"

"Aye, Captain," Rick said eagerly. "I'll see to it myself."

—SEVEN—

To Rick's profound disappointment, Consuela proved no easier to approach once housed within the crew's palace.

The manor was a genuinely grand affair, with two great wings opening off a broad central gallery. Consuela and the local girl called Adriana took chambers with the other female crew in the wing opposite his own and stayed very much to themselves even when gathered for dinner.

Rick went to bed that night frustrated and confused. An entire planet of women to choose from, and here he was longing after a girl in love with someone else. It made absolutely no sense whatsoever.

————

The change started even before he was fully asleep.

There was a sense of being drawn away, detaching himself from the bed and the quarters and the palace and the world. Not of going somewhere else, but rather of first no longer being *there*, and then of *being* elsewhere.

An instant of fog-bound confusion, then he knew. He was back.

But before the panic could set in, before he could protest that the choice had been taken from him, Rick realized that the return was not permanent. He did not know how he knew, but he was sure just the same.

He arrived at that pleasant hour just before an autumn dusk, when the world was cooling down from the day's heat, and the sky was lit with a glorious display of sunset colors. Rick looked about himself, realized he was standing in the park directly across from his house. He took a breath and did what he knew had to be done.

"Rick!" His mother's voice caught him before he had passed over the threshold. She came rushing up, her high heels tapping impatiently across the polished floor. "Are you all right? Where on earth have you been?"

"I'm fine," he replied. "It's hard to explain—"

He was cut off by a voice booming down from upstairs. "Who is that, Doris?"

"Your son!"

"Rick!" A tall and aging replica of himself came thundering down the stairs. "I've a good mind to . . . What insanity possessed you to go off on your own like that?"

For the first time in his life, Rick did not back away from his father's wrath. He did not give his best smile, he did not ease things by agreeing and giving in and going along. He stood his ground, he met his father's angry gaze, and he replied, "I've been involved in something important."

"Important!" The elder Reynolds blasted his ire. "Important! What on earth could be more important than meeting up to your responsibilities?"

"A lot of things."

"Why, do you realize the trouble I've had trying to calm down Coach . . ." His son's words finally sank home. "What's that you said?"

"I have other responsibilities right now, Dad. Important ones."

"Oh, I knew it, I knew it," his mother wailed. "He's gotten that girl pregnant."

"Mom—"

His father wheeled around. "What girl?"

"That trashy thing who came around not long ago, you know the one. She said you two had been on a date."

"Consuela is one of the finest girls I have ever known," Rick said firmly. "And she's not pregnant."

"Then she's gotten you mixed up in something bad," his mother accused, her tone rising. "Is it drugs?"

"Good grief, no."

"Now you listen to me," his father thundered. "I don't know what shenanigans you've gotten yourself into these past few days, and I don't care. I want you to hightail up to your room, mister, and get ready for school on Monday. After you call Coach, that is, and apologize for all the trouble you've put that poor man through. You've got the good name of this family to uphold, and don't you forget it."

"I'm not staying," Rick replied quietly. "I just stopped by to let you both know I'm doing fine. I'll be home as soon as I can. Right now I have to go." He turned to the door, then stopped, held by a strong feeling that something was left undone. He turned back and added quietly, "Just know that I love you, and I'm doing fine. Really."

It was the image of his parents standing there, open-mouthed and shocked into stillness by his quiet determination, that brought a smile to his face as he raced back across the park and flagged down a passing taxi. He gave the driver the address, then panicked until he felt his wallet there in his back pocket. Rick settled back, the smile still in place. Whatever had brought him back had shown the good sense to return him to his own clothes, and not left him in the uniform of a lieutenant on a Hegemony vessel.

Consuela's apartment building was just as ratty and dismal as he remembered. He mounted the stairs two at a time, pressed forward by a strange sense of urgency, which he could neither explain nor disregard. To his surprise, he found an envelope pinned to the apartment door, marked for Consuela. After a moment's hesitation he pulled it down, opened it, and read:

"Dear Consuela, your mother had a bad attack on Wednesday. The doctor says it is nothing to worry about, but he has kept her over at Providence General for observation. I try to visit her every evening after work. Bliss and I are living in a rented apartment here while we try to find a home. The number is listed below. Your mother's room number is 238. Welcome back, and call us as soon as you can. I have a million questions. Love, Daniel."

Rick refolded the letter and pinned the envelope back in place. Then he raced back to the waiting taxi and ordered the driver to hurry over to the hospital.

At the door to room 238, he hesitated. What was he going to say to her? Then he heard the muffled sound of a man's voice. He knocked and pushed through to find Daniel there and seated beside the bed.

Daniel looked up, his eyes widened, and he waved Rick inside. "This is a friend of Consuela's, Harriet. Do you remember Rick?"

Rheumy eyes turned his way. The slack muscles of her face tensed as she squinted and tried to draw him into focus. "Maybe. I'm not sure."

"Your daughter is fine," Rick said, following Daniel's hand signals and drawing up a chair. "She's doing something very important and asks you not to worry."

"There, see," Daniel said, his voice infinitely gentle. "Consuela was so concerned about you she sent Rick all the way back just to let you know everything was going to be all right."

"She's a good girl," the woman mumbled.

"Consuela is a gem," Daniel agreed. To Rick he went on, "We shouldn't stay much longer. The nurse will soon be in to give Harriet her medication." Turning back to the bed, he said, "We were just talking about something, though, weren't we?"

The woman lay as though uncomfortable with her own skin, shifting about, never still. Her words were a rambling monotone. "Something nice. You talked about something real nice."

"It is nice, isn't it?" Daniel agreed, smiling with genuine pleasure. "I was telling you how God continually sustains the universe. It is a constant, never-ending gift. Were He to stop for even a moment, everything around us would collapse into chaos."

Perhaps it was the quiet assurance with which he spoke, perhaps the strength that radiated with his words. Whatever the reason, he had a calming effect on Consuela's mother. Her erratic motions slowed, then stopped. Her eyes ceased their endless search and settled upon Daniel's face. Her forehead scrunched into furrows with the effort of concentrating upon him and what he was saying.

"Think of a hot air balloon," he said. "Without the gas to hold it aloft, it collapses into a useless heap. What is true in the outside world is also true within us. We have been given the freedom to choose for ourselves, but without God our internal world is chaos. A universe of distraught emotions and conflicting aims."

Rick watched the woman nod slowly. Here was something she could understand. An internal chaos. She clearly knew it well.

" 'My father has never yet ceased his work. And I am

working too,' " Daniel said from memory. "Those were the words of Jesus, when He was questioned about His doing good deeds on the Sabbath. It means that if we allow Him into our lives, He will work within us *continually*. Without ceasing, without holidays, without moments alone when old despairs might slip in and overwhelm us."

Rick could not help watching the woman on the bed. She looked awful and smelled worse. Yet Daniel sat there, pleasant and gentle and seeming to enjoy himself. Amazing.

As he watched, Rick found himself feeling as though Daniel's message was meant not just for the woman, but for him as well. This unsettled him tremendously. What could he have in common with a bedridden old lady?

"The old order has passed away," Daniel went on in his gentle way, "not just now and then, but for good. The new order is brought into being. This is Christ's work, granting all of us living in our fallen internal universes to become transformed. We are born anew, into a universe ruled by eternal love, eternal peace, eternal healing, eternal order."

———

Soon the nurse entered and to Rick's relief asked them to leave. He promised Consuela's mother to take good care of her little girl, then allowed Daniel to usher him outside. But the unsettled feeling did not leave. As they walked down the hospital corridor, Rick was struck with the vivid impression that this hospital visit and Daniel's message were the real reasons behind his being back.

They stopped in the hospital cafeteria for a cup of coffee. Daniel sat across from Rick and listened with singular intensity as he sketched out all that had happened. To Rick's surprise, Daniel showed no consternation over the tale, and all his questions indicated that he believed Rick entirely. When he had finished, Rick asked, "Don't you find all this a little hard to accept?"

"Yes and no." Daniel eyed Rick over the rim of his cup. "I'll tell you a story of my own when all this is behind us. For the moment, let's just say I've sort of been through something similar."

"Really?" Incredible. This guy in his business suit, the neat hair and the serious expression? Crazy to think he'd ever set off on an impossible adventure of his own. "When was that?"

Daniel waved the question away. "Later. How is Consuela holding up with Wander being taken?"

"All right, I guess." Rick squared his shoulders. "I'm helping her out all I can."

There was a piercing quality to Daniel's gaze as he sat and watched Rick, but he said nothing. Not, that is, until Rick swayed and reached for his forehead, and then came close to sliding from his chair. "What's the matter?"

"I'm not sure." Suddenly Rick felt infinitely weary, more tired than he had ever been in his life. It felt as though all the hours of all the nights when he had done anything other than sleep were all gathered together, pressing him down and enveloping him in vast crushing waves of fatigue.

Daniel leaned across the table and gripped his arm. "Are you all right?"

"I don't know. All of a sudden I feel so *tired*."

He understood instantly. "Maybe this is your callback."

Rick yawned so wide his jaws popped. "My what?"

"It's as good a name for it as any." Daniel lifted him from the chair and half led, half supported him through the cafeteria and out into the lobby. "Come on, let's go to my car."

"Why?"

"We've got to get you into a place where you won't be noticed going away." Daniel hustled him through the glass entrance doors, across the road, and through the parking lot until they came to a white Buick. He fumbled with his keys. "Slide into the backseat. There's a blanket on the window ledge, pull it up around you."

Daniel stood and watched as Rick used every last vestige of his strength to settle onto the seat, then leaned over and said, "Be sure to tell Consuela that we surround her with our prayers and our love. And know that we include you in them as well."

Consuela had so much difficulty falling asleep that she scarcely realized it when it finally happened.

All the pains she had faced in her life—the poverty, the loneliness, her mother's drinking problem—nothing compared with this. It was not so much that this pain was worse. Yet somehow all the others had been *outside* her, at least in part. This one was totally within. Totally hers. Missing Wander was an ache that sealed her heart in a sheath of stone.

This time, there was no running away to some other place. No matter where she went, this would go with her. Her love for Wander was etched into every cell of her being. She found herself wondering sometimes, if she had it all to do over again, knowing that this would come, would she still want to give her heart away? The answer was an unswerving yes. This love now defined her world, for better or for worse.

For hours and hours that night she lay in her bed, exhausted by all that had transpired, made worse by the nervous strain of missing Wander. There in the darkness she discovered that the loss and the hurt had another effect, one she had never thought possible. All the lies and the shields within herself were stripped away. Everything she was had been laid bare. She felt open and utterly vulnerable. Her personality, her character, her makeup, all were opened to her honest inspection.

There was no running away from the insecurities and the questions any longer. Hard as it was to face this with her longing for Wander, the truth that was reflected in her loneliness could not be denied. And above all the other questions echoed the continual refrain, *Who am I, really?*

She fell asleep with that question unanswered, drawn into the overly active dreams of nervous exhaustion. She spent uncounted hours chasing down hallways without end for answers she could never find.

Then she started awake with a gasp so explosive it drew her upright.

She flung aside the covers, swung her feet to the unseen floor, and searched for a trace of what she had sensed. Desperately she hoped it was not just a dream. It could not have been. It was too real, too powerful.

Then it came, an image and a message and a flavor that was all his own. She felt his nearness even while knowing that the space between them was immeasurable in earthbound terms. The message was vivid, a picture without words, given only with a single wafting note of his love and his yearning for her. Intense and demanding and precious. As quickly as it came, it departed, leaving behind a vacuum so dark and empty that the scream felt torn from her throat.

"Wander!"

–Eight–

She was looking at a box of space.

The image floated above the desk, square and stationary and dark. Dunlevy lifted a silver rod tipped with light, handed it to her, and said, "Press that little button on the side when you have the correct position. I will reorder the intensity once we have the positions. Try and remember as carefully as you can. This could be what we're looking for."

The captain interrupted, "You're absolutely positive it was he?"

"Yes," she said, and cut off further talk by closing her eyes. Arnol had alternated between excitement and doubt ever since he had been summoned. Dunlevy, on the other hand, had shown no hesitation whatsoever.

As soon as she cleared away the impatient pressure she felt emanating from the others, the image popped back into her mind. It remained as clear and as prescient as before. And still it carried that faint trace of Wander.

She opened her eyes and began to draw.

The image made little sense to her. But there was no questioning the feeling of rightness as she pressed the button and saw stationary points of light appear within the dark box. It did not take long for her to finish.

She handed the control back to Dunlevy, pointed in and said, "This one is very bright, a burning blue-white globe." She watched him make an adjustment by twisting the back of the control, then touching the indicated light. Instantly it grew to dominate the box. "Yes. And these four don't have any light. They're just round circles." Again the adjustments, as though he understood what she meant almost before she spoke. "Okay, and this one is a really big star, but not a globe like the first one. Sort of reddish orange. Yeah, that's it. These two are smaller. And this one is really bright too, but almost completely white, like an arc lamp. No, brighter than that, but smaller. Like that. Oh, and there's another little globe right next to this one." It struck her then with chilling force. "That's a moon, isn't it?"

Dunlevy nodded impatiently. "What else?"

She closed her eyes, recalled three more distant lights, added them. Took a deep breath, forced herself to hold the memory as vividly as she could, opened her eyes, and tried to overlay her mental image upon the one in the box. "I think that's all."

Dunlevy looked at her with piercing gravity. "You're sure?"

She did the exercise once more, her forehead knotted with the strain. "Yes."

Dunlevy eased up from his crouched position, turned to Arnol, asked, "Do you recognize it?"

"No," he said, his craggy features holding a sense of wonderment as he glanced from the box to Consuela and back again. "Never seen an approach like that before in my life."

"Nor I," Dunlevy agreed. "And I have spent my entire adult life studying the skies."

"Excuse me," Consuela said. "But what is it?"

"A star chart," Captain Arnol explained. "It appears that your boy has managed to transmit a landing approach for a system neither of us has ever seen before."

Dunlevy leaned closer, pointed at the shining globe that dominated the corner closest to her. "I want you to think very hard. This is crucial. Did he give any impression as to which of the planets circling this sun was their destination?"

Consuela started to shake her head, but something nagged at the back of her mind. She closed her eyes once more, and there it was. The final part of the message, held in place until she was ready and able to both accept and understand. Sent to her with an appeal so strong and so full of frightened desperate panic that she almost screamed again. Instead, she opened her eyes and stabbed into the box, her finger pointed straight at the planet with the single moon. "Here! Wander is here!"

–Nine–

Grim did not begin to describe Wander's surroundings.

The castle walls were so thick that even the air seemed imprisoned, unmoving and lifeless. The halls and chambers were cold, stern, and utterly silent. Not just void of sound; there was a morbid quality to the castle, as though every vestige of energy and vitality had been sucked out.

It was the first time in memory that Wander heard no ethereal communication. Not even a whisper.

The planet itself was not just arid. There was no water whatsoever. It baked under a too-close, too-intense sun, holding its meager atmosphere at the temperature of a roaring furnace. Its single moon was overlarge, and swept up hurricane-force winds with each six-hour revolution. The surface was utterly flat and featureless, all mountains and other protrusions having been blasted into nothingness by the dry heat and the savage winds.

The castle stood at the base of a fissure ten miles deep and half as wide. Overhead there was no sky, only a continual raging fury of sand and dust and endless gales. The castle itself could hardly be distinguished from the surrounding crevasse, for it had been carved from the very same stone. Boulders sliced from the cliff sides had been shaped into great blocks as tall and thick as ten men, erected with such precision that no mortar had been required to hold them in place. The few windows were mere slits through which little could be seen, only craggy stone and jagged cliffs and furious flaming red clouds roaring overhead.

"Enough of this time-wasting," said his escort, an impatient youth with dark, pinched features and an aggressive manner. "Let's get a move on."

Reluctantly Wander retreated out of the narrow tunnel leading to the corridor's single window. Although the outside view offered little, still there was a sense of expanse. But no freedom. The slit-window was imbedded in a stone tunnel fifteen paces long, the outer wall's thickness. Beyond the thick glass was a vista more desolate and forbidding than anything he had ever seen or imagined. Despite their density, the swirling clouds at the top of the castle's canyon were illuminated by the over-bright sun. From underneath, the furious dust clouds looked like continual blasts of fire and brimstone, a flaming curtain shutting him from all space, all sky, all hope.

Wander allowed himself to be led down the silent stone corridor by the only person he had seen since his arrival. The corridor was lined by one closed door after another, tall and impenetrable. The castle appeared as void of life as it did of sound. Their footsteps scratched and echoed down a hallway without end.

Wander had been too weak to do more than protest against his kidnapping on Avanti, and the soldiers had paid his feeble words no mind whatsoever. The diplomat had only looked his way once as they had made their final approach toward the waiting spaceship via floater. He had peered down at where Wander sat exhausted and feeble in the power-chair, and sneered, "You would do well to harbor what strength you have, Scout. You will need every shred soon enough. And more besides."

The diplomat's vessel was jet black, formed with some substance that seemed to suck up all light and reflect nothing back. They had not gone through the spaceport, but rather floated down directly alongside the mighty ship. The warriors had obeyed the diplomat's sharp command and had taken Wander to a featureless cabin, dumped him from the chair onto the floor, and left him lying there. His protests had meant nothing at all.

Wander felt as well as sensed the ship's gradual upsurge in power. He managed to drag himself into his bunk. He remained upon his back, as calm as he could make himself, knowing that he had to reach beyond his crying heart and his aching sense of loss, and *observe*.

To his surprise, the ship did not enter directly into interstellar transport.

The ship raced out beyond the planet's double moons, then began powering up to full thrusters, racing faster and faster outbound while at the same time reaching toward null-space without benefit of an energy net. Wander had never heard of such a maneuver, had not even known that it was possible. Yet as the ship's thrusters continued to build up to peak power, he understood how such a maneuver would keep the planet-bound tower personnel from sensing exactly where the ship was destined.

Then time slowed to a crawl, and the transition hit him.

It was Wander's first full-fledged transition within a starship not bound to the relatively short distances of lightways. He felt an explosion of his awareness, and at the same time a sense of controlled caution. Near to him was someone else with heightened awareness, a trained pilot whose attention was tightly focused upon the destination ahead, and yet who was also observing him. How this was possible, Wander did not know. Yet his senses, expanded by the almost limitless moment of transition, were too clear to be denied. He was being watched.

So instead of extending himself outward as he desired, he held back, caution granting him the ability to hold his awareness to what he could see without being seen. He observed the ship's direction, watched as the ship made the instantaneous transition in and through n-space, and as the ship powered down after transition, he made a very exact identification of their destination.

Perhaps because the ship's power-up did not permit an exact destination, or perhaps because they were monitored by some interplanetary defense system, they did not push out of n-space directly on the planet's surface. Instead, they hovered above and outside the planetary orbit. As the amps powered down and the sense of expanded awareness was gradually lost, Wander's final view was of a fierce identification blast, a radio signal sent at hyperspeed so that it could not easily be caught and interpreted.

Wander struggled to hold on to his sense of expanded time, but failed. The signal shot away from the ship just as his own awareness was returning to the confines of time and his cramped little cabin.

He sat and waited for what felt like hours after the ship had landed, until the cabin door finally slid back to reveal the pinched-faced escort. He wore what appeared to be a scout's robe, but one laced with slender silver threads. "You are to come with me," the young man said sharply, and led him out of the now-empty ship, through the connecting tunnel, and into an empty, endless castle corridor.

"This is your chamber," the escort said, pushing open a

stout door identical to all the others.

Wander walked forward and peered inside. Like the door itself, the room was functional and austere. "Why isn't anything powered here?"

The question seemed to catch his escort off guard. But he recovered swiftly and snapped back, "You'll find out soon enough. Your meals will be brought to you. Do not leave this chamber until you are summoned." With that he left, slamming the door behind him.

Wander surveyed the room more closely. Featureless walls, a steel-framed bed with a thin mattress, a single chair, a desk, a dim glow-lamp operating from its own battery source. It all hearkened back to some bygone era. There was a reason for this, he was sure, but at the moment he was too tired to care. Wander stripped off his robe, sprawled on the bunk, pulled the thin blanket over himself, and was instantly asleep.

He awoke uncounted hours later to find that a metal tray had been slipped through a slit at the base of his door. He ate swiftly, the rudimentary meal spiced by hunger. Obviously he was being watched, for the instant he set the tray aside, the door was pushed back to reveal the same young escort. "Here," he said, "put this on."

Wander accepted the gray-brown robe, felt the coarse material, and started to protest. But a glance at the escort's face told him the young man expected him to argue, and had already prepared a harsh retort. Instead, he turned his attention to a series of dark markings that extended out of the escort's sleeve and traced their way across the back of his left hand. "What is that?"

The escort looked down, smirked, and drew back the robe further. A tattoo of a three-headed serpent coiled up his arm, fangs bared, vicious and deadly. "It is the sign."

"Sign of what?"

"That I have challenged the beast and won."

Wander studied the pinched, hardened face. "The beast?"

"You will see soon enough." The young man drew himself up to his full height and intoned, "Are you prepared?"

Wander slipped the robe over his head and stood. "Am I what?"

"No, of course not. How could you be?" The young man spoke with the formal tones of one reciting something well memorized. "You know not what is to come."

Uncertain of how to respond, Wander stood and waited.

"You who were once a scout now have no position, for what was earned elsewhere has no meaning here. You who were once labeled and known are now nameless and of no account. You will regain your name only when it has been earned here."

Labeled. As though all that had come before was nothing. Wander felt the heat rise within him.

"Once you had friends. Now none except the one assigned this duty will show you his face, for you are nothing and no one."

Before Wander could respond, the escort wheeled about and passed through the open door. "Follow me. It is time for your testing."

Wander walked down the corridor in resentful silence. He was feeling much stronger now, and the anger surged through his frame. Kidnapped, torn from Consuela's arms, taken across the length and breadth of the empire, and now treated like a nameless nothing. Wander walked a pace behind the escort and bored holes in the young man's silver-threaded robe with his stare.

Without warning, the escort jinked and entered a tall open space. Wander hesitated, for in his befuddled state he could have sworn that an instant before there had been nothing to his left but more stone wall. The escort turned and stood waiting.

Wander stepped across the unadorned threshold and entered a chamber perhaps fifteen paces to a side, with lofty ceilings supported by great sweeping arches.

"Think you have already been tested?" The escort's words bounced back and forth within the empty chamber. "You shall soon think again."

The words sounded to Wander like a ritual chant. A thought struck him and he spun about, only to find that the opening through which they had entered was no longer there.

"Think you have a special power? A gift? Perhaps." The escort raised one arm, and slowly, silently, the entire chamber floor began to descend. Wander glanced up, saw the ceiling move farther and farther away. "Or then again, perhaps you have only the means to destroy yourself."

An initiation. He was being brought through a rite. But the understanding brought Wander no comfort. There was also a warning to the words. One which he did not comprehend.

"There are many paths to destruction," the escort went on. The floor upon which they stood descended at an ever faster rate, until the great stone walls blurred by on every side. "But there is only one to safety. Only one among the many."

Without warning the floor exited the stone passage and floated into a subterranean hall greater than any enclosed space Wander had ever seen. The walls were so far away as to be lost in shadowy haze. The floor descended across an expanse so vast, Wander's face was touched by a mild breeze.

He looked down and saw that they were headed toward a domed structure built like a ringed fortress wall, as high as it was broad. Lights flickered and raced back and forth through the ring's black depths. At intervals dark arms extended outward from the ring, like the multiple arms of some giant prehistoric sea-beast. They continued on and on until they were lost in the distance. Beyond rose what appeared to be several more of the rings, but because of the distance Wander could not be sure.

"You cannot hunt for the one right way," the escort droned, "for there is no time. You must simply *know*."

The floor settled inside the great black ring, upon a deck surfaced in the same yellow-gray stone as made up their subterranean cavern. From this perspective, the dark ring-wall with its endless flickering lights rose up to ten times the height of a man.

Beside their landing spot, in the center of the ring, rested two black chairs. Upon the table separating them sat two headsets.

Wander stared at the sets and asked, "How many fail?"

"Questions are for later," the escort replied. "But this one I shall answer. Of the six arrivals since I became the newest scout monitor, only one has passed into training."

Scout monitor. Wander followed him over to the pair of seats, knowing he had no choice. He accepted the headset, sat down, adjusted the set to his temples. No matter what, he would show these people no fear.

The escort sat down across from him, studied his face, and for the first time showed a flicker of reluctant approval. But all he said was, "Can you identify your home planet from the surrounding stellar systems?"

Wander looked at him askance. This was one of the simplest of initial tests for any apprentice scout. "Of course."

The escort leaned back in his seat and closed his eyes. "Then prepare yourself to do just that. Remember, it is your only hope."

Even before the power-up was complete, Wander knew what encircled him.

In an instant of shattering comprehension, he realized that the ring was a huge mind amplifier, larger and more powerful than anything he had ever heard of. It was powered not by a man-made source, but rather it tapped directly into the core of the planet itself. The beast his escort had spoken of was not an animal; it represented the harnessing of this tremendous force.

An instant's perception, a moment so swift as to be immeasurable, but this was all it took for him to understand the first snare. He recognized the desire to plunge into the amp, seeking to flee its awesome strength by burrowing downward.

Never to escape.

The outer measure of time scarcely ticked away a pair of seconds, but as the amp powered up, Wander's internal spectrum was caught in the same extension of time as when tracking an interstellar transit. He recognized the sense of time being split in two, one segment connected to his body and remaining fastened to the rigid structure of physical time. The other, however, was being expanded, further and more powerfully than he had ever experienced. Shattering in its power, yet familiar.

It was this that saved him.

Despite its awesome might, the amplifier worked along the same lines as a ship or control tower. Because of his innumerable forays to the spaceport, sitting and watching and being caught up in ships' arrivals and departures since the time he learned to walk, Wander was able both to allow himself to be carried along with this immense power-up and at the same time to hold on to his capacity to think.

"Seek your homeworld," the escort had said. Wander sensed the instructions were somehow the key, although he did not understand why.

The power-up continued, seconds ticking by externally while internally the vistas continued to open and broaden and extend.

And then he understood.

Before him spread out the entire Hegemony, a vast network of stars and planets interlaced by the golden paths of energy called lightways. Wander was approaching full power now, and there was no apparent limit to what he could see or where he could go.

And here, he knew instantly, lay the greatest danger.

Too easily newcomers would find themselves confronted with this power and simply expand outward with the amp's awesome reach. Undirected, unfocused, unbounded. Stretching out farther and farther until the mind simply shattered from the strain.

Search for the homeworld.

Wander began focusing the power, sectioning space into quadrants. His knowledge of star-charting was meager, but it was enough to do a roughshod partitioning. As he worked, he became aware of another mind, watching, viewing, keeping a safe distance in case Wander allowed himself to become overwhelmed. Wander forced this awareness and this threat from his mind and concentrated on the task at hand.

Then it hit him.

Did the escort actually know where his homeworld was located? With the unchecked swiftness of a mind amped to full power, Wander decided that it was a risk worth taking. The spatial segmenting continued, but now with a different destination.

The space around Avanti was identified, the star system

located, the planet approached. Wander felt the escort's awareness move closer, check his own internal status, then retreat. Somewhere in the distance this second mind turned away for an instant, in order to begin the power-down procedure.

It was then that Wander acted.

In the instant he was not being observed, before the power-down commenced, Wander sent two messages. He could not seek out Consuela, did not even know if such a thing were possible. So he simply blanketed the planet with his messages, backed by as tightly focused a beam of power as he could muster, and bound with the unspoken words of his heart.

The retreat was swift and undeniable. Wander allowed himself to be drawn back down and into the planet's bowels. In the juncture before his return was complete, he was confronted with a final awareness. The escort's attention was turned back his way, and now there was intermingled a sense of astonishment. Of cautious disbelief.

Wander kept his eyes closed as the world reformed into physical focus and knew that somehow he had done more than was expected. This was not a place where he wished to draw too much attention to his abilities, not until he was more aware of the dangers. So instead of opening his eyes, he slumped to one side and moaned. The reaction was only half feigned. He still felt the weakness from his time in the hospital. The escort moved over to him, and Wander let off one further moan.

"So you're not as special as you first seem," the escort said, poking Wander in the chest. Wander rolled his head to the other side and gave an open-mouthed groan in reply. The escort snorted. "You may be the first to have accomplished the task on his premier journey, but still the beast made you pay."

The escort tilted Wander's chair back and dragged it over to the waiting platform. As they began their ascent, the escort said formally, "Welcome to your new home, scout monitor, the only home you will ever know." As the great chamber was left behind, the escort muttered almost to himself, "May your chains not chafe you as they do me."

–TEN–

Consuela found the whole thing utterly baffling.

Ever since she had returned to join the crew, Rick had crowded her. It felt as though he was watching her every step. At first she put it off as just one more confusing notion in a difficult time. But with each conversation, with every passing hour, his feelings became clearer.

If she had not so much else to worry about, she might have even found it funny.

There would have to be a reckoning, she knew that. But she also knew that in all this alien hurry and commotion, Rick was the only link to her home. And she did not want to break this link with a careless word. So for the moment she did her best to keep her distance and hold at least one other person between them whenever possible.

Right now it was Dunlevy. The pilot sat on the airship seat next to hers, blocking her from the aisle. Rick was directly behind her, kept from trying to crowd in by the chancellor and captain, who occupied the next row forward. Dunlevy leaned forward, concentrating intently on their conversation. Consuela watched the world drift by outside her window and welcomed the relative solitude.

So much was happening. For two days now the crew had scurried with frantic haste, trying to prepare for their departure. The ship was ready, the new crew members as well trained as they could be while still on the ground. Every passing moment increased the risk of their secret coming out. Of some hidden glitch slowing them down. Of Wander being . . .

No, she wouldn't permit such thoughts. Consuela gave her head a violent shake and strived to focus upon the scene outside her window. They passed over a harsh desert landscape, not of sand but of mountains. Ochre hills fashioned by wind and heat and eons into sharp-edged peaks. There was not a single cloud, just limitless blue sky stretching from horizon to horizon, and overhead the dual suns with their eternal rainbow arcs.

Dunlevy leaned across her, squinting into the distance, frowning with concentration, shaking his head at something the chancellor was saying. Then suddenly all the crew was crowding over to her side of the vessel, leaning close to the windows, filling the air with their exclamations. Consuela searched the distance, wondered at what the excitement was about. She spotted the ship and was even more confused. It was the least impressive structure she had seen since this entire experience had begun. It looked like an overlong, skinny metal ice-cream cone, with a dark glassy dome for a top. The long tail was pierced with holes. What was more, the workers had apparently not even bothered to paint the outside. It had the raw, unfinished look of junk steel. She was in the process of turning toward Dunlevy to ask him if the ship really was ready for space, when she was struck by a half-formed notion. She turned back, leaned her forehead against the window, squinted, and gasped aloud.

The *size*.

From their altitude, it was easy to forget that these were true mountains they crossed. The ship had been erected in an open-ended valley and stood taller than the peaks to either side.

A *valley*.

As they began their gradual approach, Consuela saw how the cables strung from the two opposing peaks were not thin spider webs as she first thought, but actually were bridges large enough for trucks to drive back and forth upon. Which meant that the holes opening along the vessel's length were massive, larger than the ship they now traveled in. Which meant, which meant . . .

Consuela looked down at buildings rising from the valley floor, counted six and seven stories, measured them against one of the holes, and gasped a second time.

The ship was over two miles high.

Dunlevy glanced at her face, smiled, and said, "This is known as a gas miner, used in processing liquefied metals found in the high-density atmosphere of the gas giants. You have heard of these?"

Consuela nodded. "We have two in our own system, maybe more. Jupiter and Saturn."

Dunlevy frowned. "Again you mention planets of which I have no record." His face cleared as attention returned to the giant vessel they were approaching. "No matter. This is a perfect cover for our operation, for the gas mining ship must be both large enough and strong enough to withstand enormous combinations of atmospheric pressure and heat and turbulence."

Captain Arnol chose that moment to raise his voice, speaking not just to her but to all the gathered crew. "The ship that we see below us has been named Avenger, an apt title given our aims. As most of you know, a ship of this make is designed to descend through the gas giant's outer atmosphere, and as it drops it begins to spin. The speed of revolutions becomes so great that it forms a sort of mini weather system, almost like a submerged whirlpool. Once it has this island of relative stability established, it continues sinking down to where metals are flowing as gaseous liquids, and begins processing."

"The central pillar rising up through the undersection is laboratory, factory, and storage bins," the chancellor said, picking up the discussion. "The ship's power plant, anti-grav stabilizers, and thrusters are all located in the underbelly of the upper section."

"A highly specialized vessel, with ample space for hiding everything necessary for our actions." Arnol turned to the chancellor, his craggy features sharpened by proximity to his new command. "Although I confess I am baffled at how you could keep a full battle-ready weapons system a secret."

"Aye, sir," Guns spoke up from farther down the aisle. "This is not just ordinary defenses we're speaking of. Seems any basic inspection would uncover an attack system."

"We did so by separating them entirely from the ship," the chancellor replied as their airship began sinking down alongside the vessel. At such close quarters the ship's size became even more formidable. "May I suggest that we allow your crew to begin familiarizing themselves with the flight deck, and we will see to these other matters."

———

The black-robed diplomat was unable to hide his astonishment. "You say the new boy completed the initiation trial his very first time?"

"Powered up and began segmenting the quadrants without hesitation," Digs answered. "Almost as though he had been trained as a monitor before."

Beady eyes probed. "Why almost?"

"Because he didn't know the quadrants. He had a vague idea, but he was off by tens of parsecs. Like he was trying to draw along lines he had maybe glimpsed once in a book."

"And yet he knew," the diplomat murmured.

"What to do? Absolutely." Digs had been around long enough to have observed how the monitors treated the diplomats, mixing disdain and caution in careful doses. He stood because he had not been offered a chair, but did so in an insolent slouch. He was doing well enough to be able to count himself as one of the inner circle, whether or not he still wore scout's robes. There would be no more bowing and scraping to the likes of this desiccated old prune. Not ever again. "He didn't fight the power-up, not for an instant. Just rode the wave, caught sight of the expanded timescape, and knew exactly what to do. Split space by quadrants, more or less anyway, and isolated his goal, and honed in. Focused, fast, and precise."

The diplomat rubbed his chin for a long moment before saying in dry undertones, "How fascinating."

"Sure is." Digs did some probing of his own, hid his keen watchfulness by idly scratching an itch he did not feel. "You act as though you wanted him to fail."

"It would have been more convenient," the diplomat murmured to himself, then stiffened abruptly and focused once more on the young man standing before his desk. "That will be all."

"What do you want me to do for his next stage?"

"Take the customary steps," the diplomat snapped, irritated by his momentary lapse.

"Sure you don't want to put him under something a little more intense?" Digs pretended to be the diplomat's ally. "I mean, you want me to break the kid or what?"

The gaze sharpened into a calculating beam. "You could do that?"

"Just say the word," Digs answered, and hid his loathing with the training of one trapped on Citadel for almost four standard years. "I can break him like matchwood."

———

Rick stood at the back of the little group traversing the cavern-way on their floater and tried to make sense of the confusion that surrounded every contact with Consuela.

As they had descended from the airship, he had moved up close and said, "We have to talk."

She had turned to him, not with the pleasant politeness he had expected, but rather with a keen glance that probed very deep. Down to the layers of himself where even he felt uncomfortable. "I'm not sure that's a good idea."

"What are you talking about?" He kept his tone overly casual. "I just have something important I need to tell you."

She had spent a moment in silence, which somehow lent extra weight to her gaze, as though she were measuring him. "Come to the pilot's station when you're back."

The pilot's station was the most public spot in the entire control room. In the ship for that matter. But something in her gaze had left him certain that nothing would be gained by protesting. Rick had simply nodded and turned away at the sound of Guns calling him.

It was only now, as they continued down the winding cave, that he wondered why she seemed so much in control. This was not what he had come to expect from women. Normally control was totally his, without his even asking for it. He felt furious at the way she was treating him, leaving him both unsettled and aching for her. He didn't even understand why he felt so attracted to her.

But he did. He couldn't deny the fact. And the way she

treated him only seemed to feed the flames.

The natural cave through which they passed had been expanded into a vast series of underground factories and warehouses. Great passages opened up at regular intervals, the rock still bearing the blast-marks of hasty carvings. The air around them was filled with floaters, piled high with men and equipment and with the battering sounds of metalworking.

"We have worked under one watchword—secrecy," the chancellor was saying from his place at the floater's bow. "The same concept dominated our planning. To work on more than one ship would have aroused suspicion, but at the same time we sought to enter the battle with our identity unknown. We have arrived at, in my opinion, a rather novel solution." He nodded to the ground forces officer beside him, a stocky woman with eyes and hair of steel gray. "Take over, Engineer."

"Aye, sir." She turned to the gathered group and said, "Mining ships work on the pod system, scouting out prospective sites, ferrying men and supplies, establishing a moonbase away from the strain of gas mining. We registered this one as having a dozen multipurpose pods, then added some changes of our own."

"Battle pods?" Guns' voice rose a notch. "You armed pods?"

"To the teeth," the engineer affirmed.

The floater landed in an empty passage, unmarked save for a single pair of great steel doors. The engineer stepped down, said, "Now if you'll just come this way."

But Guns was going nowhere. He turned to Arnol, said, "Begging your pardon, Captain, but this has been tried before. Pods are suicide machines, good for bringing in a swift initial attack, but only with men deemed expendable. That's why all you see these days are robot pods, even though computer-driven actions are more predictable and the communication links slow down reaction time. With the small number of pods we're talking about here, I can't see us using them effectively against a heavily defended base, even if I were willing to see my own men go down in flames."

It was the chancellor who responded. "Your sentiments are most worthy, Weapons Officer. And I might add that they match our own exactly."

Guns turned a pained expression toward the chancellor. "Sir, I hope you'll believe me when I say I'm for this mission one thousand percent. But I'm a weapons man to the bone, and I need to go in knowing my men'll have at least a fighting chance."

"Weapons Officer," the chancellor replied, "we are hoping to avoid all casualties whatsoever."

"Then pods just won't work, sir, manned or unmanned." Guns clearly looked uncomfortable holding center stage, but his cautious nature forced him to speak. "The problems are well known. Weapons systems powerful enough to take on a pirate ship, much less a base, need a full-purpose power-pile behind them. Batteries and storage systems are dandy for a single blast, but there's no telling how many shots we'll need, nor how long a battle will last. That means sooner or later my men and I will be sitting up there, our shields down, with nothing but stout hearts to defend ourselves." He turned to Arnol in helpless appeal. "Sorry for sounding off like this, Captain, but I've got the success of this mission to think of."

Arnol looked at the chancellor and said, "When it comes to matters in their fields, I have every confidence in my men and their judgment. If Guns says a pod will not succeed here, I would be loathe to put him or any of his men in one and send them off."

But the chancellor did not appear the least perturbed by their concerns. Instead, he turned back to the engineer and said simply, "Tell them."

"We redesigned the power plant systems," she replied. "Shrunk them by a factor of thirty, worked out a different shielding, held them to almost peak power."

"I thought that was impossible," Guns said weakly.

"So does the Hegemony," the engineer replied.

"If there is anything that might assure you of our commitment to this project," the chancellor said, "it should be this and the material we used in constructing these secret pods. The resources of three planets have gone into this project."

"Now if you will please follow me," the engineer said, and ushered them toward the massive doors, which began to rumble open at their approach. Beyond the colossal portal, all was shadow and half-seen forms. But what Rick could make out left him breathless.

"Lights," called the engineer, and the sudden illumination drew a gasp from every crewman's throat.

A jet black flying saucer floated overhead.

That was Rick's first impression. But at closer inspection, he saw that the shape was more like the head of a spear. The leading edge flowed smoothly out into a flat knife-edged line, without sharp angles or any other evidence of construction whatsoever. It looked like some substance that absorbed light had been reduced to its molten state, then poured into a gigantic spear-shaped mold. There were no protrusions, no rough edges, no openings or closures or visible weapons.

Guns walked under the ship, back out, inspected how the center segment belled out both above and below in perfect symmetry, creating a central portion perhaps twice the height of a man. It was hard to tell exactly, for the curvature was so smooth and so gradual, and the material absorbed every particle of light. His eyebrows were almost in contact with his hairline by the time he turned back to the engineer. "How large a power plant did you say?"

"I didn't," she replied, clearly enjoying his reaction. "But it is capable of holding a force ten charge through three fusion bolts while maintaining full acceleration."

If possible, his eyebrows crept even higher. "For how long?"

"You would die of old age," she replied succinctly, "before your energy supply runs dry."

Arnol walked off the ship's twenty-pace length, his head upturned and brow furrowed. He turned back and demanded, "Where did you lay your hands on elemental trinium?"

"Another of our many secrets," the chancellor replied. "One of our allies is the planetary system that supplies this material for all diplomatic and battle-fleet vessels. They too suffer under the Hegemony yoke."

Guns demanded of the engineer, "What weapons?"

"Phasers, neutron missiles, improved stun-bolts, strafers," she replied proudly. "And a new form of energy lance."

"Not to mention the ship itself," the chancellor added, motioning to the engineer.

From an inner pocket she pulled out a small control console and fingered in a command. Silently the ship began to tilt, until the nose was pointed directly downward. Another command, and the leading edge was brought within arm's reach.

"Careful," the chancellor warned.

Cautiously Rick reached out a hand, touched a substance that was neither hot nor cold. He ran his hand down the edge, drew back with a startled cry. He looked at his finger and saw that it was bleeding.

"We did not know if we would be facing an atmosphere world or not," the engineer explained. "Elemental trinium can be shaped like a sword, and that is exactly what we decided to do. You will find, if you are ever forced to attack through wind and storm, that there is virtually no drag or buffet whatsoever."

Guns examined Rick's hand, gave him a handkerchief, said with eyes agleam, "The lad's bloodied the ship. I say it's his by right."

"A dozen well-armed individual battle pods," Captain Arnol said to Guns. "Split into four groups of three, attacking in utter secrecy and without any warning whatsoever. What say you, Weapons Officer?"

"A challenge worthy of our finest effort, Captain," Guns said, excitement racking his voice up taut. "A battle to go down in history."

"So say I also." Captain Arnol turned to the chancellor and gave a formal bow. "Sir, I accept the commission and the challenge."

"The hopes of our three worlds will go with you," the chancellor replied in equal formality.

"Battle pods are an ungainly name for such a fine vessel," Guns observed, his eyes still on the upended ship.

"We thought the same," the engineer agreed, "and have come to know them as Blades."

–ELEVEN–

"It looks like a Formula One race car from the twenty-third century."

"What are you talking about?"

"It's incredible." Rick could not think of what he had seen and stand still at the same time. He paced about the pilot station, ignored the stares and smiles cast his way, and talked with his hands. "I mean, the thing is a racer's ultimate dream come to life. I asked what the thing would do, you know what the engineer said? Thirty gravities. Zero to thirty gravities instantaneous acceleration. Do you know how fast that is?"

"No."

"Neither do I." His laugh had a frantic quality. "But I bet it's faster than I ever thought I'd be driving. Especially something that doesn't even have wheels."

Consuela sat, calm and untouched by his excitement. "You realize I don't have any idea what you're talking about."

"A fighter," he exalted. "The best fighting ship you've ever seen. It makes the F–14 look like something the Wright Brothers designed. I mean, this baby is a dream."

"A dream," she said, "or a nightmare?"

That stopped him. "What do you mean?"

"We are doing this to save people from years of oppression and being ravaged by pirates," she replied quietly. She sat with hands folded in her lap, her features composed in a mixture of sorrow and youthful beauty. "The hopes of an entire planetary system go with us."

"Sure, I know that," he said, but had to wonder why he felt so ashamed by her words.

Consuela eyed him with that same sense of unspoken wisdom that had so unsettled him earlier. "What was it you wanted to see me about?"

"Oh, yeah." It was with a vague sense of disappointment and defeat that he sank into the seat next to hers. "I went back last night."

"Back?" Her dark eyes opened in surprise. "Back home?"

"Yeah. Your mom's in the hospital. But she's okay, and Daniel's there with her." Swiftly he recounted his experience of the night before, glossing over the disquiet he felt from Daniel's words.

But still she caught it. "Are you telling me everything?"

He hesitated, again caught by her seeing more than he was comfortable with, then went on, "He talked about some stuff."

"Good," she said quietly. "Maybe Mom will listen to him." A fleeting shadow passed over her features, then quietly she added, "Maybe I should too."

He opened his mouth to ask what she meant, but was stopped by Dunlevy hastening up the broad stairs to the pilot station. "Ready to continue with your lesson?"

"Yes," Consuela replied, and then said to Rick, "Thank you for going by to see her. I know it meant a lot."

He did not try to hide his disappointment over their lack

of intimacy. "I doubt if she even noticed it."

"She did, I'm sure of that." She looked at him, the questioning gaze piercing deep. "I'm very grateful, Rick."

He nodded, turned away, and made his way back down to the weapons station. Her reaction was not what he had hoped, but clearly there was nothing more coming. Not now. It would have to do.

———

Consuela lay in the darkness of her cabin, surrounded by the scents of newness. The quarters were very generous, far larger than what she had been given on the last ship, and on the same level as the control tower. She had been accorded full pilot's status, at least as far as her cabin went.

She should have felt pleased.

The cabin's only light came from the console by the door, ever alert to react to her voice commands. She sighed and rolled over, tired but not ready for sleep. So much had happened. So much.

The ship's departure had been set for the following day. That afternoon, the chancellor had formally handed over the ship to Captain Arnol and wished the crew success. That evening, Consuela had heard the crew discuss the Hegemony's surprising willingness to let Arnol transport the ship. They had agreed among themselves that Arnol was granted permission for this voyage only because the Hegemony never intended him to reach his destination.

Even so she found it both pleasant and comforting to return to the disciplined routine of ship life. And there were familiar faces surrounding her, both in the control room and through the ship at large. Chief Petty Officer Tucker unbent enough to smile at her every time their ways crossed. And Adriana had come aboard as assistant to the ship's doctor.

But the same troubling doubts continued to fill the darkness. Her own honest introspection refused to give way, regardless of all the new pressures that surrounded her. Consuela found herself returning to the dilemmas and insecurities and unanswered questions about herself every time she was alone. This sense of flagging confidence made such problems as how to handle Rick even more difficult to face.

Again she drifted into sleep almost without realizing that she had made the passage, but instead of returning to an endless maze of frustrating tasks, this time she found herself back home. There, but not there. Standing outside the apartment building in bright afternoon sunlight, yet knowing that she was not seen.

Knowing that something needed doing. Knowing that she was there and observing for a purpose.

She moved forward, both of her own will and guided by some invisible force. Through the doors and up the stairs and down the hall and stopping before her apartment door. Sensing that what Rick had said was correct, her mother had indeed been in the hospital, but was now back home. Then hearing a sound that had been all too scarce in Consuela's home life, a sound so rare it almost frightened her.

Laughter.

The door moved aside as though opened by an unseen hand, or perhaps it did not move at all, only she found herself passing through what was for her no barrier. As Consuela entered she wondered about that sound she had heard, for there was little in her mother's life that brought happiness to others, and she was sure she had heard two voices sharing that strange yet beckoning sound.

And then she passed down the narrow hall and entered their living room and saw Daniel.

His suit coat was draped over the back of his chair, and

he was leaning forward in intent discussion with her mother. Consuela moved closer, knowing that somehow this was the key, the purpose behind this dream that was more than a dream.

Her mother's eyes were fastened intently upon Daniel's face. She was lying on their sofa, a blanket tucked around her. Her face looked thin, but more alert than it had been in a long time. Consuela searched her mother's features and realized with a start that they did not hold the slackness of alcohol. Which meant she had not been drinking.

Her gaze still held a hint of the laughter, which was now past, but her voice was solemn as she asked, "But how am I supposed to start praying?"

The question had a devastating impact upon Consuela. She felt shaken to the very core of her being. First that her mother would ever come to a point where she could ask such a question. And secondly because her own heart seemed to respond by asking the same question. Mother and daughter speaking as one. Asking a question that felt as though it shattered the final illusions Consuela held about herself.

"First of all," Daniel replied, his voice quiet and gentle yet intense, "you must enter into prayer seeking to know God. This does not mean that you cannot ask for things. But to pray just when you want something, only because you need something you can't obtain for yourself, is a lie. Do you understand what I mean?"

Consuela understood exactly. And she understood more than just that. She looked at her mother there on the couch and realized just how much her own transitions through life had been propelled by her hidden anger and pain and frustration. Consuela had always thought that if she kept the feelings down deep, away from where even she could see them, they really did not exist at all. But in truth the emotions had always been there. And they continued to affect her every action.

"I'm not sure," her mother said slowly, but the guilt in her voice suggested that she did.

"All of us have needs that we cannot answer ourselves," Daniel told her. "It is part of the weakness that makes us human. And these very same weaknesses help us to find God, because we come to recognize that our own strengths are not enough. That we need more than what we can give to ourselves. That we cannot find the answers on our own."

Consuela felt the winds of change blowing through her heart, clearing away the dust and the cobwebs from chambers of her memories and emotions that she had thought locked away forever. It was not by self-imposed blindness that she would find true freedom, she saw that clearly now. It was not by running away, by refusing to confront the pains that had filled her young life, that she would know happiness. It was by accepting that she could never find the answers on her own.

Daniel leaned forward, his earnestness carrying a weight that was heightened by his gentle tone. "But to turn to God *only* because of these needs is wrong. It is denying God His rightful place in our lives, while at the same time asking Him to give us what we want or feel we need. We are refusing to accept Him as Sovereign Lord, while trying to draw from His strength and wisdom."

Consuela watched her mother take in the words and felt them sink deep within her own mind and spirit. Since Wander's disappearance she had thought of praying. But she had done so only in order to have things made better. Not for God. For her own sake alone.

Yet here in this moment of devastating truth, she understood that healing did not come by asking God to do some specific thing for her. It came from *surrendering*. It came through seeking Him and knowing Him and living for Him. It came not through directing and limiting and pushing away, but rather through *accepting*.

"In prayer," Daniel went on, "our foremost aim should be to know God. To know His will, His love, His wisdom. To humble ourselves before the Maker of all and enter into His glorious presence. To accept our place as members of His family, brought to Him through the eternal gift of Christ's salvation."

He leaned back, his eyes shining. "Then the Father of all creation returns us to His fold, where we have always belonged. And in His keeping, we may ask not only for the wishes of our heart but for the gift of a peace so wonderful it truly surpasses all understanding."

–TWELVE–

"I don't understand," Wander said. "You *offered* to destroy me?"

"You're right," Digs replied. "You don't understand anything." He heaved a self-important sigh and leaned closer. "Look, anybody who makes it through the first initiation is one of us, got it?"

"I hear what you're saying." *First* initiation?

"Take it from me, anybody who meets the beast and survives is a monitor. The rest is just time and training."

Wander's new chambers were the largest he had ever had by far—sleeping quarters with geometric wall-hangings to mask the cold stone, and deep furs to cover his bed and floor. A bath large enough to swim in. And yet another room, the size of a small hall, with great sweeping ceilings and ornate bronze chandeliers, where he and Digs now sat.

And according to Digs, these were nothing compared to how the full monitors lived.

His escort, his pinched features split by an unaccustomed grin, had arrived soon after Wander had awoken. He had led Wander down a baffling series of hallways, each corridor more lavishly decorated than the last, until finally he opened a door and announced that here was to be Wander's new home.

Then he had shut the door behind them, brought a bulky apparatus out of his pocket, and swept the walls and fixtures and ceiling. He had then announced that they were safe for the moment, since Wander had not been expected to move so quickly. He had introduced himself as Digs and proceeded to tell Wander of his meeting with the diplomat.

Wander listened with a growing sense of astonishment before demanding, "Then why did you tell him you would break me?"

"Because if he thinks I'm doing it for him, he won't go looking for somebody else, see?" He examined Wander's baffled expression and snorted with impatience. "Look, you're not the first sensitive who's gotten on the wrong side of a senior diplomat. There's only one hope when it happens."

"Which is?"

"Make yourself indispensable. The diplomats may rule around here, but the monitors hold the reins. This means you've got to learn as much and as fast and as hard as you can. Which shouldn't be too hard for the likes of you. You're the first one who's ever made the whole trip from Citadel to the home planet the first time out. No wonder you collapsed. What you've got to do now is work, harder and faster than you've ever worked in your life."

"I think I see," Wander said slowly.

"Sure you do. You're a sharp kid. I'll be pretending to push you over the edge, which would really be happening with somebody else. But not you. What will then happen, sooner than later, I hope, is a senior monitor will catch wind of what you're doing and what you're learning and how fast you're coming up. When that happens, they're going to claim you as their own prize."

Digs leaned back, thoroughly satisfied with his plan. "After that, the diplomat and his minions will back off. There's always a few of the monitors who suck up to the Dark Couriers—that's what we call them, but never to their face, mind. These monitors are the ones we've got to keep you away from, see, and the only way to do it is to make them think I'm doing their dirty work for them." Digs bounced to his feet. "Ready?"

Wander found himself reluctant to face the amplifier again so soon. "You mean now?"

"It doesn't get easier by waiting," Digs replied, understanding him perfectly. "There's only one way to conquer the beast, and that's head on."

———

"One hour and counting," came the helmsman's droning call.

"Pilot powered and ready," Dunlevy responded in turn as the final check swept about the flight deck. He then turned back to Consuela and asked, "Are you sure you want to do this?"

"I have to," she replied quietly.

"For you to power up to such a level is a risk. Not just for you, but for all of us and our mission. We can go nowhere without your help."

She looked at him with eyes open to the sad determination at heart level. "I have to," she repeated.

"Very well," he sighed. He keyed his console, said in the whisper-voice used when speaking to others trained in his skills, "Pilot Dunlevy to Watch Comm."

"Communicator here, Pilot. All systems go, skies reported clear."

"Have special request. Please power down for five minutes."

A moment's pause was followed by, "Repeat that, Pilot."

"Our Talent needs to scan," he said, doing as Consuela had requested. "All mind amps must be powered off, and all high-level communication ceased."

"Ah, right." The watch communicator's tone became crisp. "Anything for the Talent, Pilot."

"My thanks. Five minutes to commence in sixty seconds and counting."

Dunlevy took off his headset, turned to Consuela, pointed at the switch in her lap. "Don't let go of that power-off control. And don't hesitate to use it."

"Thank you," she said solemnly. "I am so grateful for this."

Dunlevy cracked a nervous smile. "I think I would worry less if I really understood what you were planning to do."

"I'm not sure I understand it myself." She turned her chair a quarter-circuit so that she looked out and over the control room, signaling that she needed to be left alone. Dunlevy subsided into watchful silence.

It had come to her at the end of a restless night. Consuela had returned swiftly from her half-dream and spent many hours tossing and turning and struggling with the night's message. It was only with a sense of battling against herself and her pride that she finally gave in, exhausted and afraid, and prayed.

She had slept then, not long, but enough to awaken refreshed. As she had slid from the bed, she had realized that somehow she needed to make Wander aware of her departure. And at the same time as she thought of the problem, she conceived the solution.

"All right, Consuela," Dunlevy said quietly. "It's time."

She adjusted her headset. "Is the amp on full?"

"Yes," he said, his voice registering his concern.

"I'll be fine," she said, hoping it would be true. She

reached for the dial at her right temple and slowly began to turn.

As the power began surging in, she found herself recalling those earliest times of expansion, when there in the unfathomable distance she had sensed her own heart's yearning. As though it were out there beyond her reach and within her at the same time. Consuela shifted the dial another notch and realized that perhaps the answer was in accepting her own need for God and His strength at times such as these.

Another notch, and her mind began its expansive journey beyond the ship's confines. She shut her eyes and ears to the flight deck's humming excitement, increased the power another notch, then another, and another. Refusing to follow the easiest path, out along the lightway and removed from this planet's continual noise. Turning instead so that she raised unsheltered and unfettered into the planet's higher atmosphere, and there she hovered, pushing the dial up one notch after another, until she knew that if she increased the power by a single degree further, her mind would literally explode.

Then she let her heart cry aloud.

No words could be contained in the message, she knew that. Nothing that some monitor might overhear could mention anything about their mission, or who she was, or to whom she sent this message. It could only be her heart, and it had to be so clear that Wander, if he did somehow manage another mind-journey, would have no doubt that it was she.

She sang the tragic heart song of her yearning for him, her loss over his departure. Her wordless missive was a silver cloud of emotion, spun together with the finest web of love. A shimmering veil hovering above the planet's surface, a wordless appeal for him to come, to return, to be with her. All of this wrapped about a single thought, an anguished announcement that they were leaving the planet, saying nothing more, terrified of having someone else detect the message and endanger his survival.

Robbed of the chance to speak in comfortable words, driven to ultimate risks by her own leaving, Consuela sang to him with the open helpless vulnerability of her growing love, of her yearning to be together, and of her hope that her departure would lead her to him. She gave it all to him, her awakening passion, her unanswered longings, her undying need.

Somewhere in the vast distance of physical reality, she sensed more than heard as Dunlevy whispered the five-minute mark. Consuela let the veil go spinning away, drawing from herself one final note of love, rising higher and faster and swifter than all else that her heart had sung, flying with all the force her love could give, soaring out into the uncharted depths of her loneliness, filled with the hope of a tomorrow shared with him.

And as she returned, empty and hollowed and scared and weak, she felt the silent clarion call rise both from without and within, and sensed that somehow, even in that moment of greatest solitude, she was ever comforted, and never alone.

–THIRTEEN–

Consuela left the flight deck and returned to her cabin, drained but pleased. She had done her best. What was more, she was comforted by the sense of presence, the same feeling she had carried with her since her defeat at dawn.

She halted, her hand on the door-control. No, it had not been a defeat. Rather, her pride had been forced aside, and she had accepted her need for something more. She had been compelled to accept that her insecurities and her pains could not be solved by herself alone. But this was not defeat, not if she were accepting the truth. Consuela keyed her door open, certain that it was indeed the truth that she was finally facing.

"Consuela! Hey, great, just who I was looking for."

She turned, and the moment of internal honesty granted her the wisdom to know that it was false—both the surprise that Rick played at and the great smile with which he greeted her. He was nervous, he was uncertain, and he was ready to push their friendship over the brink of his own unfettered pride.

Consuela started to thrust him away with an excuse—

she was tired, she had just come off a difficult watch, she needed a moment's rest before returning for lift-off. But before she could speak, she saw the need to confront this now. The realization was not something that came from herself. It was a gift of wisdom from somewhere beyond herself, clear and quiet and certain.

She smiled back. "Hello, Rick. Are you settling in okay?"

"Sure, great. Too much to do. Guns has assigned me a squadron, a pair of former airship pilots. They've never been in space at all, never flown anything bigger than the craft that brought us here." He grinned, less self-consciously this time. "Listen to me. As though I've had years of the stuff, right?"

"Come in." She stepped over the threshold, called for chairs, heard the ship's monitor sound the forty-five minute mark. "Would you like to sit down?"

"Sure." As he lowered himself, his nervousness returned. His hands played on his knees, with his belt, his cuffs, and his eyes were just as active. "Look, what I've wanted to tell you is—"

"Rick," she said softly, leaning forward and catching his hand with hers. The unexpected action froze him solid. She looked into his eyes, and in that moment she understood both why it was time to face him and what she should do. The open vulnerability caused by her message to Wander was still there for her, and this allowed her to show him not the pride and defensiveness that he usually brought out, but rather the truth. The only truth that might, just might, still his headlong rush and permit their friendship to remain intact.

She saw the hope kindle in his eyes and responded with the wisdom that was still being gifted to her, a sense of knowing beyond time and self-interest, a giving of what was truly her. Her gaze steady, she said softly, "I am totally in love with Wander, Rick."

The light in his eyes dimmed as fast as it had risen. There was too much truth in her words and her voice and her eyes for him to doubt. He looked down at his hand in hers. "Then there's no hope?"

"None," she whispered. "My heart is his."

There was a long, aching silence before he sighed and straightened. The barriers were back in place now, his eyes glinting with hurt pride and anger and vanquished desire. "So what is it about him that makes him so much more attractive than me?"

Consuela found herself unable to respond with anger. She looked at Rick and saw him and his distress through the pain in her own heart. She saw how his pride had been pierced by the fact that despite his looks and his abilities and his strength, she preferred another. Someone with whom he could not compete. Someone he could not overcome, and thus win her affection. And he had lost for reasons he did not understand.

So her answer was gentle, despite his wounded rage. "Because he needs me," she said, her voice soft.

Her words penetrated to a level so deep that his own anger dissolved. "So do I," he croaked.

Slowly she shook her head. "You rely on nothing and nobody except yourself. This is the perfect setup for you. Finally you're away from your parents and everybody else you ever knew, so you can stand totally alone and be the strongest and the best. The champion."

"And that's not enough for you?"

"Wander has a different kind of strength," Consuela replied. "He is strong enough to know how much he needs me."

"I don't understand that," Rick said. "Not at all."

"I know," Consuela answered. "But it's true just the same."

Even though it hurt his pride to do so, he had to ask once more. Give it a final fighting shot. "Couldn't you give me a chance?"

Again there was the gift of wisdom, the sense of knowing more than could have ever come from herself. "You don't love me, Rick. Not really. You see the love and the connection between Wander and me, and *that* is what you want." With a gentleness she would have never thought possible, she stilled his voice before it could be raised in protest by raising one hand and placing it against his lips. "Don't say anything, please. You're hurt and you're angry, and you might say something that could keep us from being friends. And I need your friendship, Rick. Do you see what I'm saying? I *need* this."

"But not my love," he muttered.

"I know you don't believe what I'm saying now, but if you'll please, please just give it a little time, I think you will see that it is the truth. You are attracted to me because I am learning what it means to be completely open and give my heart and my mind and my love and my life to someone else."

She had to stop there, almost blinded by Wander's absence. She swallowed, took a shaky breath, and saw that even this was somehow intended, for her open confession had the effect of shaking Rick out of his pride-filled self-remorse. She swallowed again, and went on, "I hope and pray that you will find this same love for yourself someday, Rick. Because you are truly a special person. I'm not just saying that. You are strong and incredibly handsome, and I need you to lean on just now."

Again the heat pressed up against the back of her eyes, and a single tear slipped through. "But Wander is so much a part of me that loving him is as natural as breathing. And his absence is a wound that almost cripples me. So please be my friend. I need a friend, Rick. Especially now."

———

"Five minutes and counting."

"Power up," Captain Arnol commanded, his face set in lines of granite.

"Power to redline crest," the power controlwoman confirmed.

"Cast off all bonds," Arnol intoned.

"Ship free and floating," the helmsman responded.

Through the vast stretches of open transparency, Consuela watched the massive cables fall with lumbering slowness toward the distant earth. The ship was now balanced upon the tight beam of its own power.

"All instruments tracking," the navigator stated. "Departure path confirmed, destination recorded."

"Avanti spaceport control grants us leave," Dunlevy announced. Since the ship would be traveling along well-established lightways for at least the first portion of this journey, there were no formal duties for a pilot. So he stood as watch communicator and Consuela's tutor.

"Four minutes," the helmsman intoned.

The ship's flight deck stood upon the ship's crest like a vast crown, far larger than that of the ship that had brought her to Avanti, for many of the mining functions would also be controlled from this point. For that same reason the interconnected vision system, which granted them the sense of having a window to the outside, was not restricted to just the ceiling overhead. Instead, the seamless view continued down around them, with bright brass handrails marking the chamber's boundaries.

"Three minutes."

What was more, the room was circled a second time, two paces in from the handrails, sectioned to coincide with the control stations, rising like concentric circles, giving views down through the floor itself. Yet instead of seeing the next ship's level, which actually lay beneath them, cameras fitted at the base of the broad dome granted them the sense of looking down the vessel's vast tubular length. Steps leading to and from the flight deck stations spread out between these floor-based visors like segmented spokes of a carpeted wheel.

"Two minutes."

"All officers," Arnol intoned. "Sound by station."

As Consuela listened to the final station-by-station check, she looked down and through the nearest floor-visor. Faint dust clouds were stirred up along the distant desert valley floor. All human activity had vanished from sight.

"One minute and counting. All systems green."

She looked around, saw how the ship was surrounded by giant serrated peaks. Overhead gleamed a pair of suns connected by gleaming rivers of light. She strived to take it all in, to imbed it deep within her, to treasure the memory for all her days to come.

"Thirty seconds."

A voice crackled through the ship's intercom. "Avanti spaceport, watch commandant speaking. Signing off, Avenger. Good luck, and good hunting."

"Roger, spaceport. Spaceship Avenger, Captain Arnol at helm. We will be reporting when we have news worthy to report."

"Five, four, three, two, one, lift-off. We have lift-off."

"Time to hook on and begin charting," Dunlevy said quietly.

Consuela fumbled for her headset, her attention held by

the arresting vista that surrounded her. Slowly, slowly, the ship rose from its surrounding valley, picking up speed with such grace and silence that it was hard to realize, except that now the peaks were far below her, and the sky was racing through darker and darker shades of blue.

"Consuela."

"Just a minute." Through the floor visor she watched as the dry ocher patch that had once been the surrounding desert shrank and shrank and shrank until it was just one small island surrounded by great fields of white clouds. And then the clouds fell farther and farther behind, until she could look and see the entire great globe with its gently curving surface and seas and snowcaps and lights where cities were adjusting to the coming night.

Night.

The double suns with their shimmering rivers of light now rested upon a backdrop of utter black. And stars. If she turned from the dual suns, everywhere she saw stars. Great blazing ribbons of silver light streaking across the depths of space.

"Scout, it is time."

"Right with you." She spotted the pair of moons then, rushing up and past on either side, their pitted surfaces glowing with every hue imaginable, the mountains and plains and exposed minerals reflecting the multitude of shades flaring down from the dual suns.

Consuela made her feeble fingers fit the headset to her temples, glanced over, found Dunlevy staring at her strangely. "What?"

"You have never seen a lift-off before, have you?"

"On television."

"Your homeworld did not have airships, spaceports, floaters, or regular contact with the Hegemony?"

"My homeworld," Consuela replied, "did not have any

of those things and a lot of other stuff besides."

"I had heard," he said, his mind busy adjusting to this new information, "that there were frontier stations out beyond the Rim that had been lost during turmoil after the Great Transition. Planets that had reverted to primitive states and forgotten that there even was such a thing as the Hegemony." He looked at her. "Your homeworld was such a primitive?"

"That pretty much sums it up."

"So how then were you discovered?"

"I guess you could say," Consuela replied, and looked down at the swiftly shrinking globe below them, "that I just got lucky."

At the sound of the bored call, Digs pushed open the stout door and walked up to the diplomat's desk. "Ship blasted off from Avanti at the start of the current watch. Calls itself Avenger. Strange name for a giant gas miner, if you ask me."

The diplomat kept writing, his attention only half caught by the scout's report. "The sooner we're done with that blasted . . ." He caught himself and glared at Digs. "That was your report? You disturb my routine to tell me that the ship carries a strange name?"

"The planet is permanently flagged," Digs reminded him. "We are ordered to report anything out of the ordinary. The ship carries a pilot on registered home leave to Avanti, seconded with Hegemony permission for this delivery. But the ship started off by lightwave transport, instead of going direct. According to the manifest, they plan to test all systems before making a jump. And they are carrying a shipment destined for a nearby star system."

The diplomat's irritation subsided. "You say this is a new vessel?"

"First time outbound," Digs confirmed. "Never even made an interplanetary trial. Seven months behind schedule, according to our records."

"Then it seems a reasonable plan." The diplomat mulled it over. "Is this the ship that man, what is his name—Oh yes, Arnol. Is he commanding this Avenger?"

"I'd have to check the manifest," Digs lied, without understanding why, masking the fact that it was there in his pocket. Hiding his surprise that a diplomat would be interested in one particular ship's commander. "But I think I saw that name somewhere."

The diplomat showed a flicker of interest. "Any idea what cargo they will be delivering locally?"

Digs shrugged. "Usual Avanti cargo, far as I could make out. High-tech stuff, a lot of things I couldn't identify. Lot of high price tags, that caught my eye."

"Let me have a copy of their trajectory and manifest," the diplomat said, his voice lowering to an overly casual tone.

"Right." He took that as dismissal and started for the door.

"Just a minute." When Digs had turned back around, the diplomat demanded, "Just exactly what is a scout doing monitoring a flagged planet?"

"Monitor Damien handled that quadrant until this morning," Digs answered. "But he had a sudden attack of the screaming jeebies."

"Don't be insolent," the diplomat snapped.

"I don't know what else to call it when a monitor tears off his headset and goes into a weeping fit right there in the cavern." Digs' voice was overly harsh, but he was beyond caring. He and Wander had just been checking in when it happened. His skin still crawled from the memory, and the fear that it might happen to him someday. "Besides, since it was Wander's home planet and we're working from that point anyway—"

"What?" The diplomat half rose from his seat. "Avanti is *not* that boy's homeworld."

"It's not?" Digs was caught flat-footed, something that rarely happened. "I thought—"

"Go get the boy," the diplomat snarled. "Bring him to me. Now."

–FOURTEEN–

"I can direct the ship through transition," Dunlevy was saying. "I can chart the course. But only you can tell us where our destination lies."

Consuela studied his face, saw that he spoke in earnest. "You can't see the shadowlanes?"

"I knew of them only through rumors, until I met you."

Their station formed the uppermost portion of the right-hand series of rings, or starboard deck as it was known. Light came both from the stars overhead and from soft illumination encircling each ring as well as from the flickering lights on each station's control panels. The effect was both to unify the flight deck and to offer each station a sense of comfortable isolation.

Consuela continued to gaze at him. "No one else can see them?"

"No one that I know. There is endless speculation wherever pilots gather and speak freely. But never have I met someone who claims to sense them as I do a lightway."

"It's all so natural to me," she said.

"I believe you," he said somberly. "Listen. A lightway is a carefully measured route, used by Hegemony ships since the dawn of interstellar travel. They are anchored by power satellites, great banks of prisms and mirrors and focusing instruments in permanent solar orbits."

"Wander told me about that. Part of it, anyway," she said, glad she could say his name without the catch in her throat.

"For those who truly believe shadowlanes exist—"

"They exist," she said. "Take my word for it. Please."

"The best explanation I have heard for their disappearance," he corrected himself, "is that they were *made* to disappear. There was a period called the Great Transition, brought on by the training and deployment of pilots, when in the course of fifty years the empire underwent a tenfold expansion. Imagine. Ten times the number of stellar systems and perhaps five times that number of new transport lanes. A complete restructuring of the known universe."

Dunlevy raised his eyes to the stars overhead. "At such a time of upheaval, with careful planning, any number of things could be made to disappear."

"But only if the Hegemony was behind it," Consuela offered.

"Exactly," Dunlevy agreed. "By locating the shadowlanes, your friend has uncovered one of the Hegemony's darkest and most ancient secrets."

A keening pierced her along with the sudden fear of what they might do to Wander in return. She pushed it away by asking, "So what is it I am sensing?"

"Traces," he replied. "Traces so faint and so old that they are beyond the ken of every other pilot I have ever met."

Captain Arnol swiveled about and addressed Dunlevy, "I am waiting your first report, Pilot."

"Aye, Captain." Hastily Dunlevy fitted his headset into place, said loud enough for Arnol to overhear, "We'll continue your lessons off watch, Scout. Now hook in and power up."

Consuela did as she was told. They were still a full day's acceleration from the first point where the Three Planets' records showed that a ship traveling upon this lightwave had sent its final message. She knew for certain that she could not reach that far, not yet. But Arnol wanted a constant check made of the path they flew, running forward as far as she could manage. Which meant that she would never be off the flight deck for more than a couple of hours at a time. She did not mind, not really. She was busy, she was needed, and she was moving toward her love.

But scarcely had she begun to turn the dial on her headset when the entire flight deck seemed to vanish beyond the power of an incoming message.

Before she knew it, she was on her feet, screaming at the unseen ceiling overhead, "Wander! I can hear him! He's here!"

———

"Forget her!" The diplomat slammed his fist down on the desk. "Accept that for you, she no longer exists!"

"I can't do that," Wander replied quietly.

His subdued state calmed the diplomat somewhat. "You must. Be forewarned, Scout, your life hangs by the slenderest of threads."

Wander kept his eyes downcast, afraid that if he looked up, the diplomat would detect the love and the yearning and the stubborn hope radiating from his heart.

His first warning that something was amiss had come with shocking suddenness. Earlier that same day, Digs had guided him not down to the training ring where all his other watches had taken place, but over a segment of the great cavern to where a second, far greater ring rose from the yellow stone floor. This was one of seven monitor stations, Digs had explained, from which the empire was kept under constant surveillance. One of the senior monitors had already heard of Wander's success in the first trial and had wanted to meet him.

But as they had floated down inside the ring, one of the three men seated at the central station had suddenly let out a bloodcurdling shriek, flung his headset up and over the ring, and started clawing at his robes. "Home! I want to go home! Take me away, I can't stand it! No more, I beg you," and then the young man had collapsed into a sobbing heap.

The two other monitors, both older and gray-bearded, had ignored the arriving pair completely. With disjointed movements they had risen from their stations and moved toward the fellow.

One knelt beside the sobbing young man, looked at his mate, and asked, "You felt it also?"

The other man, the eldest of the trio, nodded back. "It shook me to the core, I can tell you that."

"What was it?"

"No idea," the elder replied. "None whatsoever. I have never experienced anything like it, and hope I never do again."

"I felt as though somebody had attacked my heart," the kneeling man whispered, allowing the sobbing young man to rock within his arms. "Torn it open. Told me things I never—"

The elder noticed them then. He frowned, then nodded as his addled mind struggled to focus. "You're Digs and that new trainee."

"Scout Wander, Senior Monitor," Digs replied for him, his own eyes never leaving the crumpled form.

"We have an emergency. I need you to assume monitor activities for this watch while we take care of him."

"Yes, Senior Monitor." Digs accepted the sudden promotion with no elation whatsoever.

"You are currently operating your training techniques within Vector Two, yes, of course, that is how I heard of you. Very well, carry on." He started to turn away, then stopped. "No, wait. There is a message on the table there for the diplomat. Along with a manifest. A ship left Avanti by lightway at the start of our watch. It's all there. Report in when you finish your watch." Then he turned away in dismissal.

As Digs directed their floater back toward the training station, Wander asked, "What was that all about?"

Digs shrugged miserably. "It happens sometimes, or so I've heard. The beast gets the better of somebody and tears him apart. First time I've ever seen a senior monitor break, though."

There was none of the banter that had come to signal their growing friendship as they hooked in and began the power-up routine. The training task was simple, though Wander did his best to mask the fact. Each training period, they returned to Avanti, then began working outward, tracing the lightways, learning the myriad of interconnecting lanes and stellar configurations that made up the inner Hegemony star chart. Avanti was ever the starting point, an anchor for their work. Yet because Digs was always there and vigilant at the onset of each training period, Wander had been unable to leave a second message.

This time, however, was very, very different.

The power-up complete, they made what was now a swift and steady approach to Avanti. But just as they arrived and turned away, Wander found himself overwhelmed by Consuela's love.

There was no mistaking the fact that it was she. Words were not necessary. He felt it was Consuela, knew it was she, knew it was a gift for him. A gift of her heart. And a single, fleeting, urgent message.

He felt the passion of her awakening affection, the sadness over his departure, the determination to find him, the longing hope that they would soon come together once more. All of it was there, bound together by the indelible strands of her love.

Wander felt his own heart fill to the bursting point at the same time that Digs was jerking away, pulling back, powering down. He allowed himself to return to the training station, knowing that she was no longer on Avanti, certain that he would carry her gift forever.

Digs tore off his headset, asked, "What was *that*?"

Wander found it surprisingly easy to play at calm. "What was what?"

"You didn't feel that?"

"Feel what?"

"Nothing." Digs's hands were shaking as he set the headset down on the table between them. "Are you sure you're all right?"

"Yes." Wander watched him rise unsteadily to his feet and felt a faint glimmer of hope. "Aren't we going to train?"

Digs looked at him in disbelief. "You really want to go back?"

"Sure. You said I needed to work as hard as I could. I'm ready."

"Maybe you are," Digs said, looking askance at his own headset. "I couldn't do it again now."

As calmly as his stuttering heart would allow, he suggested, "Then let me go alone."

"What?"

"It's got to happen sometime. I've seen how you order the power-up. Why don't you let me give it a try?"

Digs appeared to be having difficulty focusing on what

he was saying. "Sure, if you want. I think, yeah, maybe I'll go report to the diplomat about . . ." He glanced at the papers given to him by the monitor. Color was gradually returning to his face. "About this ship. Flagged planets are supposed to be kept on constant watch, and, anyway, what better way for him to think you're getting blasted than to send you off so early on your own." He stopped and looked down at Wander. "Sure you can do it?"

"Don't see why not." Almost there. Almost. "I just go back to Avanti, right?"

"Yeah, and stay there. We'll start mapping again next watch." Another disturbed glance at his headset, then Digs moved toward the floater. "I won't be long."

Wander watched as the yellow stone platform flew up toward the distant roof, holding back as long as he could manage, before fitting on his headset. His heart thundering with anticipation, Wander did the mental reach as he had observed Digs make, and gave a silent shout of exultation as the power-up began.

With eager swiftness he reached out and forwarded himself to Avanti. The task was relatively easy. The system only had four lightways radiating outward, and the monitor had said that the ship had left on that very watch. They had to be somewhere nearby. They *had* to.

He raced down one after the other, identified the ship on the third lightway he scouted. Felt his pulse soar as he centered in, focusing upon the ship, and sending the single word message.

Consuela?

The sudden response was all he could have hoped for, and more. The scream of joy and heartache and love and passion almost shattered his heart. He reached down, focusing as tightly as he could manage. *I'm here.*

Wander, Wander, Wander.

We may not have much time. I need to do this first. Did you get my coordinates?

A second voice broke through the emotional flood from Consuela, a clearheaded response to his query. *Pilot Dunlevy here. Yes, she heard and recorded. Perhaps you could repeat for safety's sake.*

Swiftly Wander recoded the star chart location, then added, *The transition ended just beyond lunar orbit, not on land. There was a hyperspeed radio squeal sent just after we came out of n-space. I assume it was an identification signal. I did not get a chance to make it. Sorry.*

Can't be helped. There was a pause, filled with the sweet scent of Consuela's longing, then Dunlevy was back. *Captain Arnol asks what can you tell us of surface defenses.*

Swiftly Wander described what he had seen of the raging storm and the castle's canyon. *I know nothing about other defenses, but if I can I will try to check. This place is beyond huge. I am working from a cavern big enough to hold a city.*

According to Senior Pilot Grimson, it used to house an entire battle squadron.

Wander took great comfort from the sound of the familiar names. *Where are you headed?*

Take note, came the crisp response. *Here are our trajectories as close as can be identified, given the likelihood of battle and perhaps pursuit.* Quickly Dunlevy imprinted what they knew of the pirate's stronghold. *This is at present a best-guess only. Afterward we shall make a delivery at Selanus, a planet with the following coordinates.* A swift image was passed on, showing a star system farther along the same lightway which they traveled en route to the pirate stronghold. *From there we are scheduled to deliver this vessel to Yalla. Do you know the system?*

Negative.

It is a star system not too distant from your coordinates. We have a possible buyer for our vessel there. Here is the star chart. After it was passed over, there was another moment's pause, then, *Arnol suggests you give us seven days for isolation and attack. It cannot take longer than that and allow us to maintain our cloak of secrecy. After that we shall make our delivery, then head for Yalla by direct transition.* Another pause, then, *Now that we have contact with you, Captain Arnol has decided to wait in silent orbit one-half parsec beyond the Yalla system's outermost planet for a standard day. If we hear nothing further from you, we will make directly for Citadel.*

Citadel, that is truly the name of this place?

As far as we can tell. No record exists of the star chart you have passed on. Do you have our coordinates and time plan?

Affirmative.

Arnol emphasizes that we may make better time than stated. If you are unable to make further contact, expect us when we arrive. Scout Consuela will attempt to make direct contact as soon as we break from n-space, but there will be no chance to wait and try and contact you once we arrive at the Yalla system. Our only hope is to maintain surprise. We shall attack without delay.

Understood.

Then I shall break contact. A brief pause, then, *I look forward to making your acquaintance in person, Scout Wander. Until then.*

A moment's silence, then Consuela said, *I never knew what hope meant until now.*

Or love. He reveled in her intimate presence, then asked, *Can you try to leave me more messages?*

Yes, oh yes.

Wander sent images pinpointing places where he would look. *If there is anything more you can tell me, include it there. But be careful. Others can sense your communications.*

I'll try.

He felt her reaching out, sent his own heart surging across the immeasurable distances, wasting not a second with hesitation or self-conscious doubts. There was no time. His imprisonment had never felt so complete or so void of meaning. Their hearts touched because their lips could not. They yielded to each other with a grace and a passion that left words far behind. They soared in joyful union, a new heart song lifting them beyond space and time and distance and separation, one borne by the ecstasy of shared love.

Then Wander sensed the approach of another, and reluctantly, sadly, gently, he separated himself. Needing no words to convey how he felt or what he thought. Allowing himself to be powered down, away, out of the heart's embrace.

He opened his eyes to find Digs looking down worriedly at him. "The diplomat wants to see you. Now."

Wander raised himself with a sigh, walked to the floater, watched the cavern floor disappear into the distance, yet seeing almost nothing at all.

She was with him still.

–FIFTEEN–

The diplomat glared at him across the expanse of his cluttered desk. "Every day, every hour I am tempted to rid myself of you and the risks you represent."

"I'm not a risk to anybody, Diplomat," Wander replied quietly, his eyes still on the floor at his feet.

"Of that I'm not so sure." He inspected Wander coldly. "Was there some design behind your being sent to Avanti?"

Wander's surprise was genuine. "I didn't even know it existed until we arrived."

"Perhaps, perhaps not. Even so, why did Grimson choose that particular training flight for you?"

"You'll have to ask the senior pilot," Wander replied feebly, recalling their panic-stricken departure.

"Indeed I shall. But in the meantime you will forget this girl you left behind on Avanti and watch yourself very carefully. Another such maneuver and you will find yourself terminated in the slowest and most painful manner possible. If you wish to survive this day, you must accept that the outside realms no longer hold anything for you. You have no family, no lover, no friends except those made here. In the meantime, you will be watched constantly, your actions carefully assessed. Is that clear?"

"Yes, Diplomat," he answered miserably, realizing that his chances of communicating with Consuela again had just been destroyed.

"Very well. Now get out of my sight."

————

"Who'd have thought it possible," Guns said cheerfully. "Me, traveling with a pilot and scout both and liking it. Not to mention risking my hide to rescue another. Times surely do change, eh, lad?"

"Yes," Rick said quietly. Up one moment and down the next. A hero on Avanti, lauded by his shipmates, but nothing to Consuela. Her friend. The consolation prize offered a loser. Her friend.

They traveled the transport tube down the vessel's vast central channel toward the weapons hold. They passed level after level of factory chambers and storage holds, any one of them large enough to swallow the ship that had brought Rick to Avanti and have room left over for more.

Guns caught sight of Rick's face. "What's eating you?"

"Long story."

"You had a perfect run first watch, that should be enough to cheer anybody up." Guns eyed him keenly. "Still pining over that scout?"

Grimly Rick nodded his head.

"Well, I've changed my mind about the likes of her, and I'm man enough to admit I was wrong. But I still say a warrior's got no business messing about with scouts or pilots either. They've got their world, lad, and we've ours. A man's got to hold tight to his duty. Especially before a battle."

He caught the sudden edge to Guns' voice, felt the sudden adrenaline surge in response. "You're right."

" 'Course I am. Watched too many good men go down

because their minds weren't on their weapons. Wouldn't want to see that happen to you, lad."

Their own hold came into view through the transparent tubing, and instantly Rick felt his burdens lighten. Spread out before them were an even dozen of the jet black fighters, their attendants busy with last-minute adjustments. "I'll be okay."

"Sure you will." Guns clapped him on the back as they stepped from the tube. He raised his voice and called across the vast hold, "Now where is that lazy good-for-nothing Tucker?"

"Lazy, my granny's back teeth." The beefy senior petty officer came stomping up. "Been down here drilling my boys into line and waiting for you overpaid sky divers to roll your carcasses out of your bunks."

Rick ignored the glower Guns gave in return. Their skirmishing was well known, and mostly show. His attention was already caught by the sight of his ship. *His* ship. He walked over to where his two other squadron pilots stood waiting. "Everything okay?"

"Ready and waiting," they confirmed. Both were seasoned airship jockeys and had a good ten years on him. But neither seemed eager to disagree with his promotion to squadron leader. His battle with the pirates upon the approach to Avanti was well known throughout the ship, and from what he had heard, continued to improve with each telling.

"Mount up," he said, echoing the order he had heard from Guns.

Rick walked under his own ship, which hovered effortlessly just above head-height. He nodded to the deck supervisor, who gave him a cheery thumbs-up. He then looked up and said, "Open Blade Three."

A split appeared in the formerly seamless surface, and

from this new portal sank his seat. Rick climbed on, felt the surface mold to his form, then said, "Load Knight Three."

It was Guns' idea to call the Blade officers "knights." Any battle squadron worth its mettle needed something to bind them together, he had insisted to Arnol. Something that would set them apart, make them feel special. As if they needed anything more than a Blade to make them feel special, Rick had thought, but said nothing. The contention between Guns and Tucker had erupted that very same day.

The Blade cockpit was more than spacious for one man. The view was spectacular. He was encased in what from the inside appeared to be a transparent bubble, which melded into the sweeping dark Perspex of the Blade's nose and sides. His controls were ranked on arms, which could be withdrawn or brought forward as required. Everything was functional, efficient, and thrilling.

Once again, his sense of prescient knowledge was there to help steer him through the vast array of new technology. Rick had caught on so fast Guns had assigned him as a training instructor for both his squadron and the third, taking on the other two himself. His run of the earlier watch had been the first for all of them operating as a team, and his two squadrons had far outshone those operating under Guns. The senior weapons officer had been as proud as if he had invented Rick himself.

Guns' voice sounded over the intercom. "Power up, Knights. Arm for blanks and seal your firing circuits. Then count off."

Rick fired the ship's main drive, leaned his seat back to a forty-five degree angle, drew the weapon console up and over his head. He keyed the console for blanks, which meant he would have every sensation of actually going into full battle, but all weapons would be blocked from firing.

He heard his two fliers acknowledge, then reported, "Squadron two, powered and sealed."

"Same drill as before," Guns ordered, once the count off was completed. "Target is the aft hold. Squadrons One and Three, adhere to me. Two and Four, take orders from Knight Three. Lift off in thirty seconds. That is, if the battle squadrons think maybe they can shake the lead out."

Tucker's response came growling through his intercom. "Just be glad we're on the same side, me boyo. Else me and my boys'd make mincemeat of you and them fancy machines."

"Thirty seconds it is," Guns said, the smile clear in his voice. "All together now, let's make this one count."

Outside, the safety light shifted to green, signifying that all the deckhands were behind safety doors. Rick felt his pulse hammer faster still, both from the sight of the great outer doors rumbling open to reveal the vastness of space and because of the surging currents of power that permeated every shred of his being. The Blades were wired similar to standard weapons consoles, with the extra thrill of being keyed directly into a main transport power-board. Not to mention the additional excitement of *flying*.

The two squadrons under Guns started forward. Rick checked his six Blades, was satisfied to see them conform to pattern. Behind them rested the bulky cargo transporters, refitted internally to become ground-troop carriers, all of whom operated under Tucker's command. Rick thought the squarish transporters looked like oversized city busses, minus paint and wheels.

"Waiting for you, lad," Guns said.

"Squadrons Two and Four," Rick responded. "Move out."

Steadily he glided across the hold, through the vast steel portals, and into space.

"I wonder if I could have been mistaken about the girl's sensing abilities," the diplomat mused aloud. "What if that blasted transport skipper was lying?"

The battle-hardened guard captain shrugged disdainfully. "Have the local emissary bring the captain in for questioning."

"Impossible. He blasted off with a new mining vessel scheduled for delivery." The diplomat smiled, a chilling grimace. "I've arranged for them to have a little accident en route."

"Smart," the guard captain approved. "Tie up all the loose ends. No need to have our little attack on Avanti shouted around the spaceways."

"Besides which," the diplomat continued, "that emissary is a fool. The only reason he holds that post is because of allies within the Hegemony court."

The two were sealed within the diplomat's quarters, the papers and consoles shoved aside to make room for a flagon of wine and two goblets. The warrior poured them both another goblet of the amber fluid. "How much trouble could one girl be?"

"I wonder." The diplomat drank from his heavy crystal glass. "Could she have left this Wander a message? Is that why he has been returning to Avanti? Something in that quadrant has been wreaking havoc among my monitors. Two of them are under heavy sedation at this minute."

"So I heard." The guard captain was a grizzled warrior, a man of many skirmishes and wars and medals. He was utterly pleased with this present berth, keeping sky-bound weapons poised and armed, an occasional off-planet exercise to keep his men on their toes, everything they could ask for to keep them content in their hole, and far enough away from the Hegemony to remain untainted by court intrigue. "But I thought sending such an unattached message was impossible."

"For standard pilots and communicators, certainly. But for a full Talent?" The diplomat sipped at a drink he did not taste. "There are so few of them that what they can and cannot do remains a total mystery."

"The girl?" The captain's eyebrows lifted a notch. "A Talent?"

"I was so sure it was impossible. The boy shows the potential. He did, after all, detect the shadowlanes as they passed." Another sip. "I never thought there could have been two of them together. Never. That was why I was so quick in believing that blasted Arnol when he dismissed her as a mere parasite. May the pirates soon make dust of him and his fine new vessel."

His scars and his years of service had earned the captain the rank of diplomatic courier, which meant he carried many more secrets than he ever wished to know. "So what now?"

The diplomat pondered a moment in silence, then turned and said, "I want you to go back for the girl."

"To Avanti?" The guard captain pursed his lips. "Difficult. Maybe impossible."

"It wasn't before."

"Ah, but this time me and my men, we'll be robbed of the element of surprise. They'll be ready and waiting for us."

"I don't care." The diplomat raised himself to his feet, indicating dismissal. "Contact the emissary through our channels and find out where they're keeping her. Make sure you mark the communication urgent, priority one, otherwise he might take months to reply. Once you've gained the information, make a midnight run. Avoid the spaceport entirely. Take all our available ships and the entire detachment of dragoons if necessary. But find that girl and bring her to me unharmed."

—SIXTEEN—

It was a painful night.

Without fully understanding why, Rick knew he was standing at a crossroads, and it had nothing to do with whether or not he chose to return home.

This choice involved his heart.

He knew how easy it would be for him to become the callous lover. It called to him with a plaintive familiarity. He was strong, he was handsome, he was a hero. He could have any girl he wanted.

Almost.

That he had offered his heart to Consuela and that she had turned him down was all the invitation he needed to never give himself in love again. He saw it all with instant clarity. He would become the man who gave his heart to none, who took and took and took, and gave nothing in return.

It was so attractive, this invitation, so very easy to accept. He would have a life filled with conquests, with women eager for his summons, with pleasures he could scarcely imagine. He would rise in the ranks, be showered with honors, and with them would come ever more beautiful and cultured and eager women. He would have riches. He would have fame. He would have it all.

And never be hurt again.

It called to him, this vision, and all he had to do was simply accept. The life was there for the taking. He knew it with a certainty that went beyond all earthly logic.

Yet it was with this very same clarity of vision that he knew such a choice would leave something unanswered. Some essential hunger would always go unfulfilled.

He lay there, tempted to shove the troubling visions aside and simply accept what he could so easily come to consider his due. But he did not. The quiet call of his own heart spoke to him, awakened by the love he saw in Consuela's face and gaze, a love destined for another and ever denied to him.

Yet was it really?

His pride would certainly like for him to think so. That if he could not have this woman's love, he would give his own to none. Yet the night's crystal clarity, fueled by his heart's soft yearnings, left him knowing that in truth it was not so. That were he to learn how to open his heart, he could have all, but only if he were willing to give all.

And this thought terrified him.

All his life he had made it by being tough, by holding back and striving for the top, being the loner who was constantly struggling for success. To be the best. At whatever cost. Even the cost of true affection.

Could he do it? Could he learn to accept someone into the innermost parts of his being, sharing all the hurts and the angers and the blackness that had fueled his scramble for the top? Rick struggled to push aside the eager temptations for just a moment and to examine himself with honesty.

And with honesty he realized that he could not do it alone.

It was this simple truth that troubled him most of all.

———

Two standard days later, the strain was showing. Consuela ate all her meals in the saddle, and left the flight deck only for three-hour snatches of sleep. Her rest was never long enough to be truly satisfying. Without actually ordering her to stay, Arnol continued to make it clear that he needed her there as much as possible. It was not enough to search for shadowlanes. She needed to set up a continual sweep of surrounding space, their only hope against surprise attack.

Dunlevy matched her hour for hour and never allowed her to sit a watch alone. He had numerous years of spacing experience behind him, yet he did not carry the burden of the search. The pilot did not show the pressure, save for a gathering half-moon of darkness under each eye.

Still, their searching had paid off. Three shadowlanes had been identified and marked on their computerized charts. Consuela had then powered-down long before they actually crossed the shadowlane path, thus saving herself the strain of making contact again while amped.

But they had found no pirates.

Dunlevy sat with his plate perched in his lap and a glass making a chilled puddle on the edge of the pilot's console. "I confess I felt some of the private exchange between you and Wander back there. For that I am sorry."

"It's okay," she said, too tired at the moment to feel shame over their intimacy being sensed by another, especially one she was coming to see as a friend.

"I have never heard of anything like this ever happening before," he said, shaking his head at the memory. "It is one thing to transmit a mental message formed into concrete images and words. But emotions. Never would I have thought such a thing could be done."

"Wander is a very special man," she said, blushing with the pleasure of such a claim.

"Yes, he is," Dunlevy agreed. "I am only now beginning to understand just how special." He drained his glass, gathered the remains of her meal, stacked the dishes and set them to one side. "Shall we commence?"

She made a face. "Do we have to?"

"No," he said calmly. "But if you do not, who will?"

She sighed, accepted her headset, fitted it into place, leaned back and began turning the power dial. Gradually her awareness shifted away from where she sat, moving beyond the flight deck, extending out and away from the lightway. Each time she pushed herself a little farther, extending her reach, trying to see how far she could manage to sense forward and around without losing her sensory anchor upon the ship.

Then she found it.

"Shadowlane!" Consuela called, sitting upright, not bothering to mask the tension that shot through her body. "And a ship!"

The flight deck was catapulted into action. "Yellow alert," intoned Captain Arnol, bolting from his casual stance at the rear of the control room directly into his station. "All hands, prepare for action."

The helmsman sounded the alarm, the flight deck shone with the pulsing yellow glow, then all tensed and waited. Every eye in the flight deck was upon them as Dunlevy leaned toward her and said quietly, "Are you sure?"

Consuela checked again, a swift in and out that left her nerve ends screeching. "A shadowlane and a stationary ship," she confirmed.

"Power Control Officer," the Captain intoned softly, now unwilling to shatter the moment. "Move to full shield."

"Full shield it is, Captain."

Dunlevy asked quietly, "Can you show me?"

She nodded, accustomed now to his following her out, leading him to a place he could not see himself. He in turn had the training she lacked to pinpoint the timeline.

"All right," Dunlevy said. "Let's go."

"On the ready, Navigator," Arnol ordered.

"Aye, Captain, ready to take the mark."

The incessantly angry buzzing struck her with the force of a billion metal bees. "There!" Consuela cried.

"Four hours, fifteen at . . ." Dunlevy paused, then shouted, "Mark!"

Arnol looked at the navigator. "Anywhere near the point where other ships have vanished?"

She inspected her charts. "Aye, Captain. Nine have sent their last recorded message before that point. And it matches the information Avanti supplied from the captured pirates. The pirate base should not be far off."

Though it cost her tremendously, Consuela did not back away. She had to be absolutely certain. She extended out, out, searching one way, then the other, and found it. "A second ship! They are sitting on either side of the intersection."

"Helmsman, full stop," Arnol commanded.

"Aye, Captain." A long pause, then, "Ship is stationary."

Arnol keyed his console. "Guns, there are two targets, not one."

"Two ships, aye, Captain."

"I am giving you three hours for a final trial run. Make it count, and make it good. Nothing fancy. Follow your orders."

"To the bitter end, Captain."

"Red alert in three hours and counting." Arnol switched off and turned to the pilot's station. "Join me aft for a coffee, both of you."

—SEVENTEEN—

"I want you to tell me what it is like," Arnol said.

Consuela sipped at her cup, then set it aside. Her stomach could not accept anything just then. "Awful. Like termites eating inside my skull."

Arnol glanced at Dunlevy. "That does not sound like a simple trace of leftover energy belonging to an ancient shadowlane, Pilot."

"No, Captain, I agree."

"Whatever it is, it's powerful," Consuela confirmed.

"Then it makes it doubly difficult to ask this, but ask it I must." Arnol's face was grave. "We have two choices in attacking the pirate stronghold, assuming we are successful with this first skirmish." His hands drew star charts in the air between them. "Either we can traverse the shadowlane, which was our original plan, riding down the line until we come within Blade range."

Stationing his arms as intersecting points, he went on, "Or there is a second option. Once we have completed our attack on the ships, we could travel back down the lightway. We could then cut through open space, traversing a line charted by our navigator. That might give us an extra advantage of attacking the base itself from an unexpected quadrant."

"Oh no," she murmured, the captain's request coming clear.

"I'm afraid so," he replied somberly. "The only way this is possible is if you can traverse the distance yourself, giving us a specific mark for where the pirates have their hideout."

"I would be there with you the entire way," Dunlevy assured her. "There would be no need to make the traverse but once."

"It could mean the difference between success and failure," Arnol told her. "Between losing half our Blades or more, and having no casualties at all."

He had hit her with the one argument she could not refuse. Consuela nodded once and started back toward the pilot's station, knowing she could not live with herself if she did nothing and something then happened to Rick.

Dunlevy settled into the saddle beside her. "All the way," he said quietly, "I'll be there beside you."

She nodded, her eyes already closed and one hand tuning up the headset dial. "Just hold my hand, okay?"

It was harder than anything she had ever thought possible. To begin with, the range was extreme. And traversing the shadowlane was like trying to focus at the limits of her ability with a drill biting into her brain. But Dunlevy was as good as his word, not simply traveling alongside her, but striving constantly to surround her with his confident strength. The pressure on her hand was matched by the sense that he walked with her, unaware of the way she traversed, but always there, ready to draw her back if the strain became too great.

It almost did, before she hit upon the idea of not remaining upon the shadowlane at all, but rather skipping along like a stone jumping across water. Touching it just often enough to hold to her course, then speeding along through empty space, allowing her mind and extended senses to recover from the shock. Passing farther and farther beyond what she had thought would be her maximum range.

Then she found it. "There!"

"Mark!" Dunlevy's voice was saber sharp. "Eleven hours, eleven minutes, and thirteen seconds." Instantly he began pulling her back.

"No, wait." Much as she wanted to go, to escape, to return, she had to be certain. She scouted as swiftly as she could, almost overwhelmed by what she found. Knowing she needed to discover everything possible, knowing she could not stand much more. Then, "All right."

Back more swiftly than she thought possible, but not swift enough to suit her. Returning to an almost blinding headache and a weakness so great she could hardly strip the headset from her temples. She turned to Arnol, winced at the lance of pain caused by the movement, whispered, "An ice planet. Something around it, I don't know what, a horrible buzzing." Each beat of her heart tightened the band of pain around her skull, bringing the darkness that much closer. "Four ships, I'm pretty sure. One of them is big, not as big as us, but still very large. Two banks of weapons on the surface. I don't think . . ."

She did not feel Dunlevy's arms envelop her and lift her from the seat. Nor did she see the crew rise to their feet in silent salute as he carried her from the deck.

–Eighteen–

"Do you sense anything else out there besides planets and lightways?"

Although the question was asked in the most casual of tones, Wander was instantly on alert. "Like ships? Sure."

Digs' tone turned impatient. "No, something else."

"Like what?"

"Nothing." He seemed angry that they were having the conversation at all. "I'm supposed to ask you that, but I don't know why."

Wander turned from his examination of the distant cavern floor. Watching the floater descend and ascend through the vast subterranean hall granted him his only sense of freedom. He had stopped looking through the narrow windows. Viewing across the lifeless landscape to the raging storm overhead left him with the sense of living in a prison with flames for walls.

"He's always so concerned about what you see," Digs went on, scuffing his foot across the floater's stone floor.

"Who?"

"The Dark Courier, who else?" He shot an angry glance Wander's way. "He asks a lot of questions about you.

Whether you see things that aren't there. If you talk about words I've never heard before. Every day he asks. I tell him you do good work, that's all I know."

Wander inspected the wiry young man, his pinched features, his darting eyes. "You're a good friend," he said slowly.

Digs raised his head, returned the gaze. As the floater settled into the ring, he said softly, "You're hiding something, aren't you?"

Wander continued to meet his gaze but said nothing.

Digs went over to the station and sat down. "I want to try something."

Wander followed him over, seated himself, settled his headset into place, remained silent.

"It's the only way you're going to trust me. I decided that last night. If you're the sensitive I think you are, I think it ought to work." He settled back, closed his eyes, said, "When we power up, just follow my lead."

With the surging force, Digs held them both anchored to the cavern. Instead of extending themselves out and into space, he turned *inward*.

Wander resisted the compulsion to push away. Instinctively he understood what Digs was attempting, and allowed himself to be drawn forward, down, into the other young man's mind.

He saw the turmoil and pain of a hard life. A family even poorer than his own, tied to a scrabble-earth farm on a distant outworld, the first candidate scout his homeworld had ever produced. Sent terrified and alone to a distant world, trained for less than six months, before being uprooted once more and sent here. Trapped and lonely, one of the few lower-class outworlders to be trained as a monitor. Hating his life, yearning for a freedom that could never be his. Chained and trapped and chafing in his stone-walled prison.

Wander allowed himself to return, and opened his eyes when the power-down was completed to find Digs watching him with those darting eyes. "Did it work?"

"Yes." He did not know how to express his feeling at this sudden gift of confidence, so all he said was, "Thank you."

Digs made do with a single self-conscious nod. Clearly he was feeling very raw. But also very determined. "I was right, wasn't I? You're a Talent."

"Yes," he said quietly.

"All the monitors are sensitives, of course. But I don't know if more than a handful are real Talents. Maybe not that many." He eyed Wander swiftly, then turned away. Afraid that his gift of trust would be rejected. Forced to ask, nonetheless. "Do you see that stuff he's asking about?"

"Shadowlanes," Wander said. "All the time."

Digs' gaze fastened upon him, his eyes glittering with the excitement of knowing the barriers were down. "And the thing at Avanti that shook up the other monitors?"

Wander took a deep breath and committed. "A gift from my girl. Her name is Consuela. She's a Talent too."

"Amazing," Digs breathed. "She's on Avanti?"

"She was." The risk was tremendous, but he had to take it. This was his only chance of communicating with her again. "She's on a ship now."

"The Avenger. Yeah, I reported to the diplomat about that." A worried frown. "I think they're planning something."

"They're in for a surprise," Wander replied.

"Yeah?" A fierce light came and went. "They coming for you?"

Another breath. "They're going to try."

Digs leaned across the table, his white-knuckled hands striving to etch furrows in the polished surface. He rasped, "Take me with you."

—NINETEEN—

"Consuela."

The soft voice filtered through the fog in her head. She rolled over, groaned as the thumping pain resumed in her head.

A gentle hand raised her up, fitted a cup to her mouth. "Drink this."

She accepted the syrupy liquid, allowed the hand to ease her back down, taking none of the strain herself. She waited, coasting in the half-asleep state, until she felt the pain begin to subside. She opened her eyes to find Adriana smiling down at her, with Dunlevy standing behind her.

Adriana asked, "Better?"

"Much." She nodded, glad to find the movement did not cause the pain to return.

"I would have given it to you sooner, but we thought it best to let you rest. Would you like coffee?"

"Oh yes." She struggled upright, rubbed her face. "How long have I been asleep?"

"Almost twelve hours," Dunlevy replied. "We decided it was the best thing."

"Twelve hours." She struggled to make sense of the jumble in her head. "But that means—"

"It was a total success," he replied. "The ship heaved to out of range of their sensors and sent the Blades and transports out and around for a surprise rear attack. The stunbolts were as effective as the Avanti engineers promised. The troopers boarded while the pirates were still out and captured both vessels without losing a man or a Blade."

She accepted the cup of coffee from Adriana with a grateful smile. "Where are we now?"

"According to the navigator's best estimates, less than two hours from the pirate base. They need you on the flight deck, Consuela. We must be sure the ships are on target. And we have to get a better fix on what their defenses are."

She forced herself to her feet, ignored the wave of fatigue that rolled over her, asked, "Ships?"

Dunlevy gave her a tired but satisfied smile. "We have a little surprise in store for the people up ahead."

"Final open communication," Guns said, his voice barely above a whisper, as though unseen ears up ahead might already be listening. "By the count, Knights. Run through your ops."

"Blade three," Rick replied when it was his turn. "Take out the northern generators at mark minus fifteen seconds. When the shields go, hit the upper battery after Blade Six, then strafe with stunners at full bore."

He listened to the other leaders sound off. Each Blade was acting as a separate force, spread out thin in order to blanket the entire planet. Not really a planet, more a giant ball of ice and rock and iron, probably a comet that had strayed too far from some distant sun. Now parked in permanent orbit, haven to a pirate force that formerly had six ships by present count.

Two of them were now in their hands.

"Hit on the mark, Blades, and hit hard," Guns ordered, when the sound-off was complete. "Tuck, ready at your end?"

"Aye, armed to the teeth and champing at the bit."

"You know your attack points."

"We'll be hitting them on the money, don't you worry."

"Right." This close to the mark, neither professional had time for rivalry. "Captain, all systems are go."

"Strike hard and fast," Arnol said. "Good luck, warriors."

"Thank you, Skipper. Full alert, Blades. Silent running from here on in. Senior Weapons Officer signing off."

Warrior. Rick focused on trailing the second captured pirate ship, holding himself in tight position just clear of its blast. The captain had called him a warrior. He felt the surging power of guns armed and ready, the Blade's energy tuned to the maximum and connected to him through circuits so tight he could truly call the enormous force his own. All questions and doubts were put aside in the adrenaline-surging moment. Warrior.

Through the transparent visor he made visual contact with the target. It was a top-heavy globe, glinting black and evil in the starlight. The pirate ship he used as a shield matched it perfectly, an awkwardly constructed battleship never meant to leave deep space, with weaponry jutting from every imaginable portal. The pirate crew were locked in one of the Avenger's lower holds, the transfer made after the vessels had been secured and the bridge powered down, so that none of the enemy ever saw who had attacked and overpowered their vessels. Tuck's ground troops were now being transported in the requisitioned ships, armed to the teeth and prepared for null-grav battle.

Rick flew in perfect tandem, his relatively tiny Blade

nestled between two massive cannons, and watched the ice globe approach. He checked his chrono, counted off the seconds, then on the timepoint shot forward like an impatient greyhound. He sensed more than marked the other Blades surging forward on tight schedule.

He had the generators locked on target when his internal alarm squealed as a ground-based cannon began tracking him. But too late. He fired the first phaser, powered up, fired again, shouted as both blasts struck home and the globe's shields shimmered once, then disappeared.

The cannons faltered in their tracking, then resumed hunting using alternate power. But Rick's squadron were in place, and the cannons were melted with two neutron missiles before they could get off their first shot.

Then disaster struck.

The largest of the pirate vessels entered into combat with Guns and another Blade, but while struggling to deflect the attack and launch missiles of its own, a rear hold disgorged a dozen misshapen robot attack-pods.

"Enemy pods!" Rick broke formation, raced forward as the first sent a bright flame shooting toward one of the Blades. "Knight Four, disengage and help Guns!"

"Busy," came the gasped reply. "Cannons located aft of Tuck's attack point."

"Blade Seven here," came the terse reply. "Engaging mother ship."

"Engaging pods," Rick said. There was too much risk of striking another Blade to launch a phaser or missile. He channeled all his power to the energy lance and roared to the attack.

A flaming sword seared the blackness ahead of his ship, a continual beam of fiery power. Without pause or hesitation he rammed straight through the first robot pod, scattering wreckage in every direction. A sharp swerve, turn, and another pod became a cloud of expanding metal.

"Blade Three!" Guns roared at him. "Rear shield!"

He canceled the lance, sent all power surging into a second protective barrier at his back, felt something slam into him with such force his Blade was sent spinning uncontrollably. He pulled back into controlled flight, saw he was too close to the mother ship, so instead of trying to disengage he refocused the secondary shields forward, rammed the drive to full power, and struck the ship with the full force of thirty gravities' acceleration.

There was a shrieking blast of friction energy as the two shields collided, then he was through, his Blade slicing the vessel like a knife through butter. Out the other end, no time to turn and inspect his handiwork, no time, for ahead lay two further drones, lances at the ready.

Rick shouted in defiance, switched power back to his lance, and raced to the attack.

The first robot pod's operator clearly did not expect the outnumbered single vessel to charge, and hesitated just long enough for Rick to mount over its sword and dive. But the second was cagier, operated by a seasoned fighter through comm-link, who raced forward and would have made a kill had Rick's reactions been a millisecond slower. But he managed to deflect the first thrust, slammed forward in an attack of his own, then made the mistake of wincing as the lances engaged in a deluge of fiery sparks.

The pod had intended this, for without an instant's hesitation it continued the swing, around and around and accelerating to a force that would slice Rick's Blade in half. But as the lance descended with terrifying force, another Blade appeared from nowhere, lance blazing, and smashed down upon the pod, blowing it away.

A breathless Guns demanded, "You all right, lad?"

"Yes," Rick panted. "Thanks."

"Tuck here," came the growled report. "Station secured. Communications destroyed. Ships under guard. Call in Avenger."

"Avenger here," Arnol said, his voice clipped with tension. "What are our casualties?"

"Ground troops report all intact."

"Blades, sound off," Guns ordered.

One by one the ships responded, their exultation louder with each man. There was a moment's silence before Guns said, his voice ringing with pride, "All hands accounted for, Skipper."

"Arnol here. Outstanding, warriors. You have just made history. Congratulations."

–TWENTY–

Consuela had the flight deck almost to herself. The skeleton crew, the only others in the control room with her, remained at their stations with little to do. They were two days from landfall on Selanus, and no further shadowlanes had been detected crossing their path. At Selanus they would halt long enough to deliver their load of trade goods, just as their manifest declared, and then make the n-space jump, guided by Dunlevy, for the Yalla system.

They had made good time since returning to the lightway, and would arrive at Selanus well within their margin of believable error, especially for the vessel's maiden voyage.

The pirate vessels had been crammed to the brim with every person found on the ice-bound globe. The Avenger crew had made the transfers through sealed passageways so that none of the prisoners could identify the attacking vessel. Then their drives had been melted down. They had been linked together, and were now being towed to the intersection with the lightway by two of the Avenger's sturdy troop carriers. Avanti had been notified and was sending one of its few remaining vessels to make the pick-up.

Then the globe had been mined with its own stash of weaponry and blown to smithereens.

Consuela checked the chrono. Three hours until the ship's brief downtime came to an end. In the meanwhile, most of the crew enjoyed a sleep approaching coma. But she had slept all she needed to. Besides, another task awaited her.

She fitted the headset into place and gradually began increasing the power-gain. She allowed her senses to expand outward, then focused upon a single point on the lightway, the next juncture where Wander had said he would search for a message.

There she began weaving another heart song, but this one was very different from the first. There was triumph this time. And determination. And righteous anger, and fierce pride in both herself and all the others with whom she had struggled. And longing. And yearning. And hope. And love.

And three words.

I am coming.

Gavin Newsom is the forty-ninth lieutenant governor of the state of California, following two terms as mayor of San Francisco. He was the youngest mayor of San Francisco elected in more than a hundred years. Newsom has founded seventeen small businesses in the San Francisco Bay area since graduating from Santa Clara University. He lives in the Bay Area with his wife, Jennifer Siebel Newsom, and their two children.

Praise for *Citizenville* by Gavin Newsom

"We need more open, innovative government to connect with citizens and win their trust. But it can be hard to know how to talk about government innovation in a way that is exciting and inspiring. Through lively stories and engaging quotes from famous digerati and less-famous policy entrepreneurs, Gavin Newsom's new book, *Citizenville: How to Take the Town Square Digital and Reinvent Government*, does just that. . . . *Citizenville* offers both an impassioned plea for more tech-enabled government and a tour d'horizon of the ways some governments have begun using technology to good effect. . . . A fast-paced and engaging read."
—*San Francisco Chronicle*

"Newsom is essentially calling for a complete redesign of the system that dictates how government handles information, and he has specific ideas on how to achieve such a transformation. . . . A passionate and well-reasoned argument for a new style of government that would treat the citizenry not just as spectators but as collaborators."
—*Booklist* (starred review)

"The book remains fresh and lively with Newsom emerging as a persuasive, if fast-talking, progressive proponent focused on how best to 'radically rethink the relationship between citizens and government.' . . . Empowering, motivating."
—*Kirkus Reviews*

"Gavin Newsom is helping to lead a new generation of government leaders who think like entrepreneurs—and who understand that technology can transform the way citizens interact with government, just as it is transforming the way we live and work. *Citizenville* offers a guide for how people can take charge of their government and their futures." —Michael R. Bloomberg, former mayor of New York City; founder of Bloomberg LP

"Gavin Newsom is a clear-eyed public servant who has never been satisfied with the status quo. *Citizenville* makes a fascinating case for a more engaged government, transformed to meet the challenges and possibilities of the twenty-first century, and where technology brings the critical tools of our democracy closer to its citizens than ever before." —President William J. Clinton

"Lieutenant Governor Gavin Newsom offers a real discussion of how we communicate and engage with the people and institutions around us—and how government can catch up, or risk getting left behind."   —Cory A. Booker, U.S. Senator

"Newsom's ideas are powerful: Why can't government enjoy the same disruptions that happen in the technology industry every day? *Citizenville*'s prescriptions form the basis of a much-needed software upgrade for our democracy."
                                        —Jeremy Stoppelman, cofounder and CEO, Yelp.com

"As a serious business guy, Gavin Newsom figured out smart new ways to run his wine businesses. As mayor and lieutenant governor, he led the way in rethinking how to govern. Now, as an author, he puts that knowledge and creativity onto the page, showing us what we citizens must do to greatly improve the way our government runs. *Citizenville* is a serious and realistic look at how to change the nature of government forever."   —Craig Newmark, founder of Craigslist.com

"*Citizenville* is nothing short of a call for revolution. Gavin Newsom, one of the most tech-savvy politicians in the United States, shows how our government has dropped the ball on using exciting new technologies—and he reveals how we can fix the situation and bring governing power to the people. In the midst of the social-media revolution, Newsom serves as a guide for how to people can take charge of their government and their futures."
                            —Peter H. Diamandis, chairman, X PRIZE Foundation; executive
                            chairman, Singularity University

"Gavin Newsom is one of the most tech-savvy elected officials in the United States. With *Citizenville*, he provides a blueprint for a government that can tap into the creativity, innovation, and transparency that define digital and social media, and makes the case for using all the tools at our disposal to improve our government—and our lives."
                            —Arianna Huffington, founder and editor in chief, *The Huffington Post*

"*Citizenville* deftly combines Lieutenant Governor Gavin Newsom's keen understanding of technology and his insight from years in public service. The result is a book that offers ideas for bridging the gap between a plugged-in citizenry and an out-of-date government."   —Marc Benioff, chairman and CEO, SalesForce.com

"The Web is a virtual city already. Web-based services, adroitly deployed, can massively improve physical cities and the dynamics of governance, as Newsom shows. His experience as an innovative and popular mayor of San Francisco gives his book particular substance."
                            —Stewart Brand, creator of the *Whole Earth Catalog*